WHEN TOMORROW COMES

*with T. Davis Bunn

JANETTE OKE

WHEN TOMORROW COMES

BETHANYHOUSE
MINNEAPOLIS, MINNESOTA

Published by Bethany House Publishers
A Ministry of Bethany Fellowship International
11400 Hampshire Avenue South
Bloomington, Minnesota 55438
www.bethanyhouse.com

Printed in the United States of America by
Bethany Press International, Bloomington, Minnesota 55438

Library of Congress Cataloging-in-Publication Data

Oke, Janette, 1935–
    When tomorrow comes / by Janette Oke.
        p. cm.
Sequel to: Beyond the gathering storm.
    ISBN 0-7642-2556-1 — ISBN 0-7642-2555-3 (pbk.)
    1. Canada—Fiction. I. Title.
PR9199.3.038 W52 2001
    813'.54—dc21
                                                                    2001002454

With deep appreciation
to God
for His unfailing
help, guidance, and answers to prayer
in every area of my life.

He is great—
and He is good.

JANETTE OKE was born in Champion, Alberta, during the depression years, to a Canadian prairie farmer and his wife. She is a graduate of Mountain View Bible College in Didsbury, Alberta, where she met her husband, Edward. They were married in May of 1957 and went on to pastor churches in Indiana as well as Calgary and Edmonton, Canada. Edward currently teaches at Rocky Mountain College.

The Okes have three sons and one daughter and are enjoying the addition of grandchildren to the family. Edward and Janette have both been active in their local church, serving in various capacities as Sunday school teachers and board members. They make their home near Calgary, Alberta.

CHAPTER ONE

The wind awakened Christine, slashing branches against the heavily iced window and flinging snow crystals with unbridled strength at the log sides of the small cabin. Down the mud-brick chimney it sounded a mournful tune, like some mythical being. Without opening her eyes, Christine knew the day would not be a pleasant one. But she smiled in strange contentment and snuggled deeper under the warm blankets of her bed.

The muffled cry of the northern wind took her back in years—more a sensation than an actual memory. It was not fear she had felt as a child as she'd listened to the howl of the wind on a winter's morning. Nor frustration that she would now be snowbound. No, it was a sense of coziness. Of contentment. She had spread out her favorite picture books before the popping pinewood fire, her toes tickled by the soft fur of the bearskin rug on which she lay. She could almost smell those morning breakfasts of hot porridge and feel her tummy rumble.

Thinking back those many years, Christine felt almost like a child again. Safe and protected and warm and loved.

It was a delicious feeling, to be wrapped tightly about one like her heavy woolen Hudson's Bay blanket.

Putting aside her reverie, she stirred reluctantly. She couldn't help wondering what would be more pleasant, pulling the covers up to her chin and listening to the relentless but futile cries of the furious intruder who seemed intent on inflicting its will on the occupants of the small home, or climbing from her bed to watch it spend its fury from the safety of her bedroom.

The raw power of the storm reminded Christine that her parents, longtime inhabitants of the North, had once again outsmarted nature's worst. No matter how it struck and fought and fumed, they were warm and safe. The cabin walls that her father had constructed for his family were still stout and strong. The small lean-to on its east side was stacked high with pine and birch logs. The morning lamps were trimmed and flickering brightly. She knew the kitchen would already be warm and fragrant with the smell of brewing coffee and cinnamon toast.

At length Christine could not resist. She swung her legs over the edge of her bed, intending to ignore the chill of the room as she fumbled in the semidarkness for the robe she had flung over a nearby chair the night before.

Tying the robe around her as she left her room, she could see the light from the open fire in the main room and a sliver of pale yellow from the kitchen doorway. She headed directly there, knowing exactly what she'd find.

Her father would be seated at the table, a cup of steaming coffee already in his hand. Her mother would be at the big iron stove, stirring a pot of the inevitable hot porridge. A small stack of toast would be tucked in the warming oven while the porridge was being served. The dog, head on paws, would be stretched out on the rug by the door—just in case someone should decide it was safe to risk a venture outside.

Christine's mother turned at the light footstep. "You're up early," Elizabeth noted with a smile. "Thought you might sleep in. This day's going to be one for staying close to the fire."

Christine nodded and crossed to the room's lone window. With the tips of her fingers she scratched at the layer of frost. "I heard the wind. It was cozy under the covers, but I couldn't resist getting a look at the storm."

Wynn stirred. "You never could," he commented with a small shake of his head. The words were spoken as a statement, but there also seemed to be the hint of a question lingering there. What was it about storms that seemed to draw Christine?

"We never had a real good one all the time I was in Edmonton," Christine said. Her voice sounded almost wistful, even to her. "Oh, it snowed. Lots. And the wind blew. But it never was able to make much headway among all those tall buildings. I never did hear it howl and cry like it does here." She couldn't help but add a little chuckle at the irony of those words and the longing she still felt for that kind of storm.

Elizabeth half turned. "You like that sound?" She visibly shivered.

Christine peeked through the opening she had managed to scrape through the rime on the pane. "I guess I do." She chuckled again.

"Well, at least I don't have to be worried now about your father. I used to lay awake praying half the night, worried sick."

Christine turned from the window and the swirling whiteness, the lashing tree limbs. Yes. She too remembered. She had worried many a night as well. As much as Elizabeth had tried to keep her fears to herself when Wynn was out in a storm, Henry and Christine had both known when their mother was uneasy and anxious. Christine recalled

Henry's valiant attempts to put Elizabeth's mind at ease. *"Dad's used to storms. He knows what to do."* Their mother would smile and nod and suggest popping corn or playing tic-tac-toe, but the haunted look never really left her eyes.

Christine tied the belt of her robe more securely and crossed the room to the corner basin to wash for breakfast. She also was relieved, more than her mother knew, that her father was not out on the trail today with the temperature continually falling and the bitter wind frosting a thick white rim on the fur of his parka. Christine's eyes sought Wynn's.

"Do you have to go anyplace today?"

He nodded. "Yes, but not for another two hours."

Again Christine's eyes went to the window, which still showed little signs of morning light. "So . . . why didn't *you* sleep in?" she asked, her voice teasing.

"Habit."

"And you?" She turned to her mother.

"I have to get up to fix Habit his coffee," Elizabeth jested in return.

Wynn chuckled. Christine knew that he made the morning coffee almost as often as her mother did, but she let it pass.

"You both waste good sleeping hours," she scolded good-naturedly.

Wynn shook his head. "We don't waste them. They're perfect for quiet times. We read. We talk. We just . . . tune up for the day."

Elizabeth was pulling another bowl from the cupboard. "Want to join us for some porridge?"

"What kind is it? I don't like—"

"I know what you don't like. It's oatmeal. No rye."

"I'll have some."

"Get yourself some cutlery and a cup."

Christine moved toward the cupboard.

"And maybe you'd better make a couple more pieces of toast," her mother instructed. "I wasn't counting on your being up so early. The strawberry jam is in the pantry."

A strengthened gust made the small house shudder. Even the dog lifted his head and whined.

"Oh boy—if I don't have shingles to replace after this storm, it'll be a wonder," Wynn commented wryly. "It'd like to strip things down to bare boards. Haven't heard such an angry wind since I don't know when."

Christine carried her cup and the coffeepot to the table. She refilled her father's cup, poured for her mother and herself, and started back to the stove. It was true. It was an angry wind. But it felt so good to be safe and warm. In some strange way she felt favored. Special.

"My . . . I do hope they aren't getting this storm down on the prairies. I'd hate to think that Henry—"

"Now, Mother. Henry's quite able to look after himself. He's well trained in survival and knows . . ."

Christine tuned her father out but could not hide a smile. The role had now been reversed. Her father was trying to assure her mother about their son, not the son maintaining that their father would be all right in the storm.

Wynn reached out a reassuring hand to grasp Elizabeth's as she lowered herself to the chair beside him. She forced a smile and a nod, but Christine noticed that, once again, the worried look did not really leave her eyes. Her mother's fingers curled around the hand that held her own as though clinging to the promise that had just been spoken.

"Has Henry called?" asked Christine, taking the chair on the opposite side of the small table.

"Not since last week."

"I thought he said he'd let us know as soon as he and Amber decided on a wedding date."

"He did. So I guess they haven't decided yet."

Another gust of wind rattled the windowpane.

"I hope they don't expect us to travel in this." Christine's eyes went to the window.

"This will blow itself out in no time. Always does," answered her father.

True, the storms did not last long. But when one held you in its icy grip, it seemed as though it never intended to let you go again.

"Is it actually snowing? Or just blowing around what fell last night?" Christine wondered.

Wynn chuckled. "It's hard to tell. I took the dog out earlier, and you couldn't see two feet in front of you. Part of it was the darkness—but even in the light from the windows, I still couldn't see."

"I guess I won't be leaving today," Christine mumbled under her breath.

Elizabeth looked up, her eyes wide. "You weren't planning—?"

"No, not really," Christine quickly reassured her mother. "But I really do have to go look for a job. I can't just sit here and—"

"I thought we'd agreed that you'd wait until after Henry's wedding."

Christine shrugged. "You did suggest that. But Henry doesn't seem to be in too big a hurry to set his date. I can't just sit here and sponge off you and Dad."

"You aren't sponging. We like to have you with us. Your company more than makes up for the little that you eat. It's been wonderful to have you help take in the garden and clean out the root cellar and rake leaves and . . ."

Christine smiled as the list continued. It was nice to be wanted at home. But she was grown now. She had experienced what it meant to earn her own keep. She really needed to be out of this cozy, comfortable nest, out on her own.

In spite of the warmth of the kitchen, though, she felt a chill as she thought about heading back to the city. She really was not a city girl. She loved the openness, the freedom of the big sky. Nature—even in its fierceness—was one with her soul. The city seemed to drown her in its haste and closeness and rushing humanity.

"Will Mr. Kingsley give you a reference?"

This brought another chill to Christine's soul. Was Mr. Kingsley, her former boss, still angry that she had refused to marry his son? If so, would he be fair? She had been a satisfactory employee. No—even more than satisfactory. He had preferred her work to the other secretaries in the office. Surely he would not jeopardize a future position merely out of spite.

But Christine was not sure. Perhaps she would be wiser not to risk asking the man for a reference.

"I don't know," she answered her mother, her voice sounding low and strained.

"Well, you got your first job without a reference. I'm sure you can again."

Her father seemed quite confident that she'd have no problem obtaining employment.

"I wish there was someplace here. . . ." Christine did not finish the thought. The wind seemed unable to disturb it, leaving it hanging there for each one around the table to mull over once again. They had discussed it before in the attempt to think of some means of employment for Christine in their little town so she would not need to leave the family once again. "Even if you moved into a place of your own nearby," Elizabeth had said, "though you know you are welcome here for as long as you wish. . . ." But each time the exercise resulted in failure. There seemed to be nothing for Christine in the small town or surrounding area.

"Maybe you should accept Aunt Mary's invitation to join them in Calgary," Elizabeth said now, seemingly fully occupied with spreading marmalade on her toast.

"But it's so far away from home."

"At least you'd be with family. And the train—"

"The train is pokey. It stops in every little town along the way. I thought I'd never get to Calgary last time. Then I still have to—"

"I know." Elizabeth sighed. "It's hard. There are just too many miles to separate us."

"I need my own car, that's what. Then I could—"

"Mercy me." Elizabeth flung up her hands. "Then I'd never get any sleep. With your own car—all on your own—driving all over the countryside. Why, I'd never have any peace of mind."

"Oh, Mother."

"It's true," Elizabeth defended herself. "It's bad enough having Henry off in one of those—and him a man. But you. What if a tire went flat or—?"

"I'd change it."

"How could you. . . ?"

"With the jack. They all have jacks. You just—well, I watched a man change one once. It didn't look so hard. Any woman could."

Elizabeth lifted her eyes to the ceiling and threw up her hands again. Wynn chuckled. Outside the storm still howled.

"Would you rather have me out with a dog team?"

The question was asked teasingly, but Elizabeth did not accept the bait. "Yes, I guess I would. At least the dogs don't get flat tires or suddenly quit, or . . . or boil up and shoot out steam or get stuck in mudholes or snowdrifts."

Christine laughed in spite of herself. "But you used to worry about Dad when he was off with the team."

Elizabeth's expression admitted she'd been caught, but she refused to concede. "That was different," she argued.

"Different how?"

"Well, it wasn't the dogs I was worried about."

"What, then?"

"Some . . . some drunk or half-crazy man with a knife . . . or a gun. Some . . . some sudden storm, or river or lake with rotting or eroded ice. Lightning strikes that started tinder-dry forests on fire. That sort of thing."

"Mama," Christine announced. "I think you are just a worrier." But she said it with love, not condemnation, in her tone.

Elizabeth's response was to rise and refill their coffee cups. Christine watched her mother fondly. She knew her mother had tried over the years to take each concern to God in prayer. It was not hard to pray about one's fears and doubts. But leaving the burden with God was sometimes a more difficult thing. Elizabeth had told Christine once that she kept taking her worries back. Working the difficulty through her heart and mind again. Fretting when she should have been relaxing in her faith. She said she'd had years of practice, and yet . . . yet . . . she wondered if she was improving in her trust level—or getting worse. Christine had given her a hug and told Elizabeth she couldn't answer that, but she did know her mother had been an example to both Henry and her over the years of what it was to trust deeply in God.

Now Wynn admitted, "I guess I might worry some, too, thinking about you out on the roads alone in an auto. Those driving machines seem to—well, need a man's hand. At least up here in wilderness country."

Christine stared at her father. Wynn had never been one to designate what was or wasn't suitable for each gender. Her face must have shown her surprise, for Wynn hurried on. "Not that a woman can't do those things—change tires, fill radiators, and all that. But it just seems to me that she shouldn't have to. It's hard, dirty work. Not much suitable for clean skirts and soft hands."

Before Christine could respond, her father continued, "It's like this here war."

The war. Yes, Canada was now at war. Christine felt another chill. True, it didn't seem real, and true it was many miles away. On another continent, in fact. Yet the fact remained, their country was now officially at war. Christine, along with many others, had been shocked by the September 1, 1939, newspapers, which carried the stark and frightening headlines. Germany had invaded Poland. The next day the papers screamed out in bold print that Britain had declared war. Canada, an independent country, had followed suit one week later. Young Canadian men—and some women—were rushing to enlist and join the cause. Christine had found herself wondering if that was what she should do. Defend her country. Be part of the troops going off to stop the enemy. She had not dared to mention that thought to her parents.

Suddenly it felt as if those chill winds had finally managed to find their way into the small kitchen. Christine saw her mother shiver, and she unconsciously pulled her own warm robe more closely about herself.

"I can understand why the young men are anxious to defend their country—all that we believe in. If I were younger, able"—Wynn's eyes inadvertently dropped to his injured leg—"I'd want to go myself. But the young women? That just doesn't seem right to me somehow. The mud and muck of trenches isn't the right place for women."

"But they aren't in the mud and muck," protested Christine. "They are in the dispensaries and canteens and offices. They—"

"The horrors of war still reach them. There's no escaping it."

"How did we get off on this . . . this morbid subject?" Christine protested. "It was a perfectly good morning, and now, here we are, discussing the war."

A perfectly good morning? The wind howled and tore at everything in its path. The snow whipped and beat on the sides of the small cabin. The temperature had dropped dangerously low, making the wind chill unfit for man or beast. Yet the fire still crackled, the coffee steamed in the cups, their stomachs were full, their feet warmed in snug slippers. They were safe in their small world.

"Until this conflict is over, it's going to affect everything we think or do," Wynn predicted. It was a sober thought. "I lost another young officer yesterday. He says he has to go or he'd not be able to live with himself. I understand that. I'd feel the same way."

Christine knew that many young Mounties shared the opinion. Would Henry? But he was engaged to marry Amber. Would he now just walk away from her and her little Danny? Could he?

"Did you know that John Beavertail and Wynn Ermine-skin have both enlisted?"

Christine had not known. Both young men were from village families that had embraced the Christian faith. Both had been educated in her mother's small schoolroom and were to have made a difference for their people. The Ermineskins had even named their baby boy after the Mountie they so admired. Wynn was not a name used among the Cree until her father had earned their trust. Christine felt fear clutch at her stomach.

It wasn't fair. It wasn't right. Why did this man—this Hitler—think he could march out and take over the world? Why? Why didn't God just strike him down? It wasn't fair. Why did good people have to die? Why would young men—and women—be called to give their lives to stop such evil?

Christine pushed away from the table. "I'd better get dressed," she said as her excuse, but really she just wished to get away. To try to escape, in some way, the presence of the faraway war that seemed to hang in the air like a pall, holding the entire country—the entire world—in its evil grip.

Someone needs to stop him, she found herself thinking as she fled to her room.

Then a new thought. *That is exactly what they are trying to do—all the young men and women who have rushed off to enlist. Gone to offer up themselves—their very lives if need be—to try to halt this wave of evil across the ocean.*

Why did she think she could just stay at home and enjoy the world as she had known it? Shouldn't she go too? Was her life more precious than the others who had already gone? And yet...?

A sudden feeling of fear and dread gripped her heart, and her face flushed with shame. She might talk big. She with her feelings of what a woman could do if she put her mind to it. But she was a coward. She did not wish to go. She would hate the muck and mud of war that her father had described. She did not wish to face the possibility of death, of an enemy bullet ripping through her flesh.

When she reached her room she did not dress as she had stated but flung herself facedown on her bed. The chill of her heart was far greater than the chill of her unheated bedroom. *God,* she cried, *how many others are going through this ... this anguish? How does one know if it is right to go—or stay? I want to pray—to beg—for safety. That you'll keep those I love here. Protected from the evil. But is it fair? Is it right? I don't know. I just don't know. Who, then, will go? Who will stop this madness? This desire for power? The wickedness of war. It isn't right.*

Even as she prayed, Christine knew the world had never been fair. Or right. Not since the day Adam and Eve had tasted of the fruit of the garden and turned loose all of the fury and hate and evil of the wicked one. There were always those who fought against him. There had always been those who were willing to pay the price of resistance. True, it wasn't fair—but it was so. And she—like every other human who had walked the earth—had to make up her own mind as to when and where she was to take her stand.

CHAPTER TWO

As her father had predicted, the blizzard soon passed, leaving a world of shimmering white. Huge drifts of snow piled up against the sides of the cabin and blocked the paths to the outside well and the shed that held wood for the fires. The brightness of the sun reflecting off the masses of white crystals made it difficult to face the outdoors without squinting. Christine, bundled warmly at her mother's insistence, worked against the mounds of snow, clearing a path between buildings and supply sources. It was good to be out. Good to have to use strength and muscle against a force of nature she could actually conquer. Shovelful by shovelful she was winning her own small war. Gradually the inner turmoil was also subsiding, though she knew she was a long way from finding the answer to the conflicts in her heart and mind.

Nearby the dog romped through the drifts, leaping and springing about to send fluffy whiteness spraying out like thick foam. The next moment he lay and rolled, pushing his back and head as deep into the mounds as he could, wriggling and writhing as though to bury himself in its coldness. Christine could not help but laugh at his antics, like a child at play.

The kitchen door opened and framed Elizabeth as she wiped her hands on her apron. She called out, excitement making her voice shrill, "Henry's on the line."

Christine was quick to toss aside the shovel, removing mittens and stomping snow from her boots as she reached the doorway.

"Christmas," Elizabeth was saying as Christine pushed past her. "They've decided on Christmas."

Christine did not bother to pull off her boots. Time on the phone was precious and expensive. She would not keep Henry waiting, paying for minutes that profited nothing. Hurriedly she grasped the receiver. "Hello."

"Chrissy. Hi. Henry here."

He needn't waste his time informing her of what she already knew. But then she wasted time by asking foolishly, "Where are you?"

He chuckled. "Where I'm supposed to be. Why?"

"You sound so ... so close."

"It's often like that after a good storm. Air seems clearer."

"There's no crackling at all," Christine observed further. "I can't believe—"

"Forget the weather," Henry interrupted. "I've more important things to talk about."

"Mom said it would be Christmas," responded Christine, pulling her thoughts in check.

"Christmas."

"That's wonderful. But ... soon."

"We didn't want to wait. Saw no reason why we should. Besides, Danny is anxious—"

"Don't blame poor little Danny," teased Christine.

Henry laughed, a joyous sound. Christine had never heard him so happy. She felt a happiness and relief of her own. If Henry was to be married at Christmas, it meant he was not intending to rush off and enlist. He'd not do that to Amber and Danny. Her relief made her feel weak.

"Amber would like to speak with you," Henry inserted into her whirling thoughts. There was a moment of delay as the receiver was passed along.

"Christine. I wish we could chat in person about our wedding plans instead of hurriedly over the phone," came the warm voice, "but I'd love to have you as my bridesmaid. Would you?"

Christine felt her heartbeat quicken. "I'd love to."

"I'm so glad."

"What . . . what do you wish for me to wear?"

"I'm going to wear a suit. I thought you might like to wear one too. Something you can wear again. You may choose the color. I'm making mine out of a . . . sort of a creamy white."

"Will Henry be in uniform?"

"Yes. And his attendant."

"His attendant. Who is that to be?"

"One of his young officers. Laray."

"So he'll be in uniform too," repeated Christine, though that question had already been answered.

"Yes. But don't worry too much about trying to match the uniform. Pick something you like. That you'll get use out of later."

Though it was not spoken, there was the war again. One could not even plan a wedding without taking into consideration that the war might rage on and on, making each purchase, each dollar spent, carefully weighed. Who knew when one might be able to obtain another new suit?

"Thank you," murmured Christine before Amber expressed her own heartfelt thanks and handed the receiver back to Henry.

"Now—I have another request," Henry picked up the

conversation. "This one might need a bit more consideration. I . . . I do want to take my new bride on a bit of a
honeymoon. I was wondering . . . since you aren't working
at present, would you be able to stay down here and care
for Danny for a week?"

Christine loved Amber's little boy dearly, but before she
could even work through a possible response, he hurried
on. "I don't need your answer right now. Think about it.
We'll understand if it doesn't work out. Amber's folks
would be glad to have him, but her mother works, and I'm
afraid a rambunctious boy is a bit much for her dad at
times. We thought—"

"I'd be glad to stay with him," Christine said quickly.
"It'd be fun."

"You're sure?"

"I'm sure."

"It won't cut into your job?"

Christine laughed. "Henry, I don't have a job."

"But you might—"

"Not now. Not with a good excuse to wait. I'll look for
a new job after Christmas. Mother has been trying to keep
me anyway."

"Then it's settled."

"You can count on it."

"Great."

"Fine."

She knew he was about to hang up, and yet she wished
to hold him for a bit longer. But what could she say? The
call already had cost him considerable money.

Reluctantly she was about to say her good-bye when he
spoke again.

"Chrissy? How about coming down early? Help Amber
with the preparations. Get to know Danny a bit better so
he'll feel more at home. You'd have to batch with me, but
I've got this extra room."

"I'd love to," she responded, anxious that he might change his mind before she could respond.

"Terrific!" He sounded genuinely pleased. "When?"

"I'll talk to the folks. Let you know."

"I'm glad, Chrissy," he said. "I'll look forward to it."

"Me too," she responded just before hearing his good-bye. The line began to hum in her ear. Slowly she returned the receiver to the cradle and turned to face her mother. "He wants me to take care of Danny while they are on their honeymoon," she explained. "He . . . he says for me to come early so I can help with the wedding and get to know Danny better. . . ."

She wasn't sure just how her mother might react. But she watched as the face before her brightened with pleasure. "That will be nice," Elizabeth said. "So nice for you and Henry to have this time together before he is married and has a family to care for. That will be so nice. It's good you haven't found a job. Then you wouldn't be able to go. I'm so glad—"

"I'm glad, too, that I'm free to go," Christine said. "I'll love having this time with Henry—and little Danny. But I do need to look for work. I've procrastinated long enough. You've always said that procrastination was right next door to sinfulness. I must shake myself out of the doldrums and get on with life. I must."

Elizabeth reached out a hand and brushed back a stray wisp of hair that had dislodged itself from Christine's woolen cap. She nodded. "Right after Christmas and the wedding," she said. "That will be soon enough."

Christine thought she read relief in her mother's eyes.

"So when do you think I should go?" she dared to ask.

"What did Henry suggest?"

"Well, nothing specific. I said I'd talk it over with you and Dad."

"I don't suppose you'll want to be there for too long a time."

Was her mother backtracking—trying to find a reason to hold her longer?

"It's the middle of November," Christine began. "The wedding is little more than a month away. If I am to be of help to Amber, I need to go fairly soon, I'd think." She found herself feeling a bit defensive.

"We'll have to get you to Edmonton to catch the train. The roads will be difficult right now after the storm."

"They'll clear them out."

"Yes—but it'll take a while."

"Dad will know. He gets the reports."

"You're dripping," Elizabeth pointed to Christine's wet boots. She wondered if it was a real concern or a means of distraction.

"I'll wipe it up."

"No, you go finish your job. I'll wipe it up."

Christine pulled her woolen mittens back on and moved to the door. "I think I'll take the dog for a run as soon as I've finished."

"Isn't it a bit chilly?"

"It will do us both good."

Elizabeth did not argue further. "Just make sure you are back in time. Your father likes to eat at twelve-thirty sharp."

"I'll be back."

Christine closed the door firmly and reclaimed her shovel. She had almost finished digging out from the storm. She would not keep her father waiting for the noon meal. In fact, she decided that the walk with Teeko would take her to his office. She would have time to discuss some things that were troubling her as they crunched home through the snow together. There was so much on her mind, and even though she had been sincerely praying for direction, she felt an older, wiser head could give her sound advice.

Her father was just stepping from the small office, fastening his parka firmly about his chin, when Christine and Teeko made their appearance. "This is a nice surprise," he greeted her, pulling on deerskin gloves. "Couldn't you stand being cooped up any longer?"

"I didn't really mind the cooped-up part," she responded. "I just thought a walk would do us good."

He nodded and moved down the steps to join her.

"Henry called."

She had his immediate attention.

"I hate to steal Mother's thunder. She'll be so eager to tell you all his news herself."

He nodded again.

"So don't ask me about Henry's wedding plans—okay?"

"Okay."

"But whenever he plans to be married, he has asked if I will care for Danny while they are on their honeymoon."

"And will you?"

"I've said yes."

"So that means—unless he is being married today or tomorrow—that you'll not be looking for a job immediately?"

"Right."

Wynn nodded.

"He also asked if I'd come early," Christine added. "Spend some time helping Amber with wedding plans."

"And you said?"

"I'd be glad to."

"So—when do you need to leave? Do I have to get out the dog team?"

Christine knew he was teasing. "I said I'd talk with you and Mother."

For a moment there was only the soft sound of the

snow beneath their feet and the occasional bark of Teeko as he imagined something hidden in the snow-draped bushes at the side of the trail.

"But you're anxious to go?" He had always been able to read her so well.

"Sort of."

"Then how are we going to get you there?"

"I thought you might have heard reports on the roads."

"I did," he nodded. "It is going to take several days to get them clear."

"How many is several?"

"At least a week, I'd think."

"Would I be able to go then?"

"Yes, unless another storm hits."

Christine nodded. There was always the threat of another storm. The very thought made her feel restless. She loved her home. Her parents. But in truth she did chafe at being confined to their small cabin day after day. When she'd been able to work outside during the fall, raking leaves and taking in the garden produce, her days had been full and productive. Now she felt her tasks were done. It was not like it had been when she was a child with a picture book. Neither was she content now to sit by the winter's fire with patchwork squares in her hands. She needed to be up and out, and it seemed there were few reasons to take her from the warmth of the flaming logs.

"Are you getting anxious to be back in the city?" Her father's question surprised her.

Christine firmly shook her head. "No. Not the city. In fact, I wish there was some way—something I could do—that I'd never need to go back. I like it out here—in the open. I'd love even to go back up north. I . . . I felt more at home there than any other place I've been. I love the North. But it seems that there is very little for a girl—a single girl—to do there. I don't think I'd be too good on a trapline. I can't stand to see the poor animals caught. That was the one thing I never did like." She shuddered at the memory.

"You could become a doctor. They always need doctors."

"But it takes so long."

"You could run a Hudson's Bay post."

"They are already taken."

"Teach, then. I expect that the government will soon have schools in all the villages."

"Dad, I'm not a teacher."

"String snowshoes?"

Christine realized her father was teasing now. She tossed her head and shot back, "They string their own. Not an Indian worth his salt who can't string a snowshoe."

"Guess you'll just have to make do with the rest of the province, then. Cities, towns, farms. You'll have to learn to be content."

Christine cast a sideways glance at the tall form beside her. "I could always marry a Mountie."

That brought his head around. He looked at her wordlessly to see if she was joshing, then nodded. But he made no reply.

They were nearing the path that led up to the kitchen door. Teeko ran on ahead, ready to meet them on the step. Christine could already see her mother's outline faintly through the kitchen window where the heat from the morning sun had freed the window of its coat of frost.

"It's not such a bad idea," she said softly, pursuing the issue a bit further.

"It's not a bad idea if you went for the love of the Mountie—not for the love of the North," responded her father just as softly, using the broom to sweep the snow from her boots before he tackled the snow on his own.

Christine had no reply.

"I suppose Christine told you the news." Elizabeth quizzed as soon as the two of them entered the kitchen.

"She said Henry called. She wouldn't tell me about wedding plans. She said you'd want to do that."

Elizabeth looked surprised but pleased. "It's to be at Christmas."

"This Christmas?"

Christine knew her father would have known which Christmas. He just wanted his wife to have the fun of informing him.

Elizabeth chuckled now. "Of course this Christmas."

"From my observations about weddings," Wynn noted with a raised eyebrow, "doesn't seem to give much time to get ready for it."

"They don't want to wait. Henry says it took them so long to finally come to an understanding that they don't want to waste any more time. So they have decided to get married on Christmas Eve."

"Well, that sounds good. Hope the storms hold off so we can make it."

Elizabeth looked dismayed at the very thought of missing her only son's wedding.

"I talked to Mary this morning," Elizabeth said quickly. "She suggested that we come a bit early and spend a few days with them. Then travel on down together."

"That would be nice," agreed Wynn, slipping out of his heavy jacket and placing it on the peg by the door.

"Christine has been invited to go early. Henry wants her to give Amber a hand."

Wynn had already heard most of it before, but he showed interest in the plans. "Good idea. I'm sure Amber will be busy. Running a business doesn't leave much time for fancy preparations."

"Oh, I don't think the wedding will be too fancy. The boys will be in dress uniform, and Amber plans to wear a suit. She had a formal gown at her first wedding. One gets more practical the second time round, she said. Especially with a war on."

Christine turned from the conversation to remove her heavy boots and place them on the thick rug by the door.

Elizabeth went to the stove to spoon the stew into the serving bowl. "Christine, could you get the biscuits from the oven, please? I've set the plate for them in the warming oven."

Christine washed her hands at the corner basin, handed the towel on to her father when she was finished with it, and reached for the oven mitt. The biscuits smelled wonderful. She suddenly realized just how hungry she had become. Exercise and fresh air had a wonderful effect on one's appetite. Even Teeko had his nose in his food dish and was hungrily devouring the contents.

CHAPTER THREE

The next morning Wynn sprang the unexpected proposal on the two women. "Why don't you travel down together?"

"Together?" Elizabeth sounded as surprised as Christine felt.

"Henry has asked Christine to come early. Mary has invited you."

"Us," corrected Elizabeth. "Mary has invited *us.*"

"Us. But I can't leave as early as you can. Like you two were saying, you need to get to the city and choose some material for Christine's wedding suit and get it sewed up. You can do that. Spend a few days in Calgary getting all that going; then Christine can go on down to Henry's and you can relax and spend some time with Jon and Mary until I get down there."

Elizabeth and Christine both listened carefully to the logic of his idea.

"Do you think we could?" Christine asked her mother.

"I hate to leave your father for such a long time. I don't see how—"

"Nonsense. I'm perfectly capable of looking after myself for a couple of weeks."

"It would be more than a couple weeks if we were to leave very soon."

"A month. I'm quite able to manage on my own for a month."

"But I—"

"Oh, let's do it, Mom," Christine exclaimed. "It would be so much fun. We could shop and visit and maybe even take in a concert or something."

"For a girl who doesn't like the city, you sure seem to be able to come up with things to do there," Wynn teased.

Christine flushed. She had not planned to act so enthused.

"When would we leave?" Elizabeth seemed to be warming to the idea.

"The end of the month, I would think," Wynn suggested. "I could join you a few days before Christmas, and we'll stay on until the new year. That'll give you a full month away."

"I don't know . . ." Elizabeth began again. "The roads can be so iffy this time of year."

"You're going to have to travel over them one time or another if you are going to be at Henry's wedding," Wynn reminded her.

"I suppose I—"

"Of course you can."

Christine felt like tossing her hat in the air had she been wearing one. It would be good to do something different. To stir about instead of being confined with not much to do day after day.

From then on their days were taken with plans and preparations for their departure. It seemed to Christine that Elizabeth spent an unreasonable amount of time baking and cooking and laying in store all manner of things for

Wynn to eat while on his own. "Mama, he will never be able to eat his way through all of this," she chided from time to time, but her words did nothing to slow Elizabeth down. More and more tins and pails and containers were carried out to the "back kitchen," as Elizabeth called the small room behind the cabin. In winter months everything placed in the back kitchen was frozen solid in a matter of minutes. It was perfect for storing items that needed freezing, but no good at all for use as simply a cold room. Now Elizabeth prepared meals by portion sizes and placed them in containers where warmth-seeking mice or marauding squirrels could not get to them. Wynn had only to draw one out, thaw it, and heat it for dinner. Everything was labeled with careful instructions. "Remove from back kitchen three hours before needed." Or, "Heat in open kettle until simmering," or "Be sure to remove wrapping before placing in hot oven."

Christine often smiled, but she said nothing. She knew her mother had to be assured that her father would be well fed in her absence.

At long last the cooking and baking were finished, and Elizabeth turned her attention to the journey. "Do you think I should wear my gray suit or the navy?"

"On the train?"

"Oh no. I'll wear the brown on the train. To the wedding?"

"You won't get a new one?"

"Me? My, no. I hadn't even thought of that. There is nothing wrong with the gray—or the navy. Either would be perfectly suitable."

Christine nodded. Either would be suitable.

"Why don't you take them both along and then decide once you're in Calgary," she suggested.

"But I hate to pack both."

"You may need both."

"Whatever for?"

"Well—if we go out on occasion. To dinner—or a concert. Then there is church each Sunday. Do you want to have just one thing to wear the entire time?"

"No. No, I guess not. But it does seem rather extravagant to take two for such a short time."

It was a reminder to Christine of how long it had been since her mother had visited the city.

"What else do you plan to take?" she asked instead of arguing further.

"My black skirt and the navy stripe and a mix of blouses and my cardigan. Then I thought I would take my crepe dress. My newer one."

Christine nodded. Elizabeth's "newer" crepe was already four years old.

"That sounds fine," she responded. "But I do think you might wish to have both suits."

"I suppose you're right." Elizabeth still sounded reluctant.

The day finally arrived when they were going to Edmonton to catch the southbound train. Christine had been very aware that her mother's eyes had been on the skies for the past days. Like Christine herself, she knew what another winter storm could easily do to their plans. But though an occasional snowfall came their way, it was never enough to delay their departure. The wind did not blow hard enough to send more than shivering snow mists scurrying about the yard.

Elizabeth's last moments at home were spent informing Wynn of where to find what and how to cope with the contrary kitchen stove. "The oven gauge does not work properly," she informed him. "So don't count on it. It must register five hundred degrees if you wish the heat to be at three-fifty."

"I'll manage just fine," Wynn patiently assured her once

more. "There's enough food to last me into the summer, and I thank you for each delicious morsel. By the time that wedding comes, I won't be able to get into my dress uniform."

"Pawsh," retorted Elizabeth. Wynn had never gained a pound in all their years of marriage. It was she who had to watch her weight.

After good-bye hugs and kisses and plenty of promises, they were tucked into the cab of the truck beside the driver, who was making his regular trip to Edmonton and often welcomed passengers. Elizabeth craned her neck to watch as they pulled away, and she waved one last time just as the truck turned the corner onto the highway. Christine fervently hoped that her mother would not become teary eyed.

But once they were on their way, she straightened her back, smoothed one black-gloved hand with the other, and turned to Christine with a smile. "It's rather an adventure, isn't it?"

Christine nodded.

"We'll stay overnight at that Edmonton hotel."

"The King Edward?"

"Yes. The King Edward. Your father has made all the arrangements."

Christine nodded again.

"I haven't stayed in a hotel for I don't know how long."

"Have you missed it?"

"Missed it? Of course not." Elizabeth paused a moment. "Still . . . it will be rather nice."

Mr. Carter shifted the lumbering truck into first gear.

"You know what I look forward to the most?" Elizabeth whispered to Christine.

Christine cast a sideways glance at her mother, whose eyes were shining with excitement over some anticipated pleasure. "The dining room? Eating something you haven't needed to cook?"

"That will be nice, I admit. I think I'll order something totally—exotic." Elizabeth was smiling now. Just thinking ahead to the adventure was becoming fun.

"Like?"

"I don't know. Maybe a beef steak."

"Mother, that's not very exotic," Christine laughed.

"Well, it will be a change from moose and elk and venison. It'll taste quite exotic to me." Elizabeth seemed to muse over the possibilities. "Maybe I'll even order turkey . . . or oysters. Oysters—that's it. It's been ages and ages since I've had oysters." Elizabeth appeared pleased with her choice.

"But what I am really looking forward to is the deep bath—where you can stretch right out in the tub and just soak and soak in all that wondrous warm water. If it starts to get cold, you just let a little out and run some more in. Oh, I can hardly wait."

"And what am I to do while you are spending your hours in the tub?" Christine asked.

"Whatever you like."

Christine laughed. It *was* going to be fun. She was so glad her father had suggested it.

———

Their driver delivered them directly to the hotel and handed their luggage to the navy-coated attendant, who greeted them with a bow and a smile. "Welcome to the King Edward. Right this way, ladies," he said with just a bit too much enthusiasm.

He insisted on hovering over their two suitcases as Elizabeth penned her name in the register, and then he was leading them once again. Their room was on the fifth floor, and Christine would have liked to walk up the richly carpeted stairway just to check out all the halls on the way.

But the man ushered them to an elevator and waved them inside.

"So what brings you to the city? Christmas shopping?" His eyes were on Christine, but his words seemed to be directed toward Elizabeth. Christine thought it a bit forward of him to ask their business.

But Elizabeth answered without reserve, "We're only stopping for the night here. We travel on to Calgary tomorrow. We have family there. We'll spend some time with them before going on to my son's wedding."

Really, Mother, fretted Christine. *He has no reason to know our whole history.*

"That's nice," the young man responded, but his eyes still had not left Christine's face. She found herself flushing. What right did he have to study her so openly?

"Only tonight?" This time he was definitely speaking to Christine. "I'm off in an hour if you'd like to take in a show . . . or something."

Christine could not believe his nerve. She did not even deign to answer. Just gave him a glance of dismissal.

He shrugged. She assumed he had been turned down before.

The elevator bumped gently to a stop, and the door opened, allowing their escape. The young man managed to jingle their room keys in hands filled with luggage. He soon opened their door and, with a wave of a practiced hand, bid them enter.

"The dining room is on the first floor to the left. Dinner is served from five to eight each evening. They will begin serving breakfast in the morning at six. The lunch hour—"

"We will not be here for the lunch hour," Elizabeth stopped him. "Thank you for . . . for seeing us to our room." She dropped coins into his gloved hand and took possession of the open door. He bowed his way out, and she closed the door as soon as she could.

"Cheeky young rascal, isn't he?" she said as she turned back to Christine. "Imagine him asking you out when you don't even know him."

Christine shook her head and crossed the room to lay her coat on a chair. "Well," she joked, "I guess it would have been one way to put in some time while you're lounging in the tub for the evening."

Elizabeth tossed a glove her way. "Talk about cheeky," she said, shaking her own head. "You are almost a match for him."

They both laughed.

———

The dining room was not able to supply Elizabeth with her oysters. "It's the war, you know," said the dark-suited waiter. "We are unable to bring such items in on the trains. It seems that the train cars are all used for transporting troops and supplies right now."

Christine wondered if it was the truth or a bald lie to excuse their shortcoming. Elizabeth masked her disappointment and ordered duck instead.

To make up for it, she told Christine, she ordered cherries jubilee for dessert and drank four cups of the rich, strong coffee.

"I'll never sleep tonight," she said almost girlishly. Christine was sure she had never seen her mother so . . . so unmotherly. So relaxed, and enjoying herself.

"The soak in the tub will relax you."

"Yes. Yes, it will. I just hope I don't fall asleep right there. You'd never manage to get me off to bed."

"I'd add a bit more hot water now and then."

They laughed at the exchange and excused themselves from the table.

"Let's walk up," suggested Christine. "I want to see how

they have furnished and decorated all the halls.

"I'm too full to walk," protested Elizabeth. "I'd never make it up five flights."

"Then you take the elevator. I'll meet you at the room."

"But we've only one key."

"You take it. You'll be there first. I'll knock."

Elizabeth nodded and headed for the elevator. Christine began the long trek up five flights of stairs. She did not rush but enjoyed each new floor with its rich, fine furniture and pieces of artwork. Heavy velvet curtains graced the wide windows at the end of each hallway and shimmering candelabra sent prisms of light over the deep wine-colored carpeting.

It wasn't until she was on the fourth floor that she saw anyone, a man and woman just leaving their room. They seemed to have been arguing about something and quickly hushed as Christine approached. The woman shot an angry look her way, but the man avoided eye contact with her as he fumbled with the key in the door lock. Christine did not bother with a greeting. She hurried on by, only glancing at the picture of the English countryside that hung near the elevator door. She moved toward the exit sign that announced her next flight of stairs and continued on to the fifth floor. But her little journey had been spoiled by their hostility toward each other and toward her.

Her mother answered the door at the sound of her knock. "There you are. I was beginning to worry."

"I dawdled. There was so much to see. You've never seen such magnificent paintings."

"Perhaps we should walk down when we go for breakfast in the morning. It's much easier to walk down than up."

Christine nodded. She did hope they would not cross paths with that couple again. She had the feeling that their mood would not improve with the coming of a new day.

"I'm surprised you aren't in that tub," she noted.

"I had to wait to let you in. Remember?"

"Sorry."

"There's plenty of time. We've the whole evening to ourselves."

The whole evening. Christine wondered if it might become a bit of a bore. She hadn't even brought a book or some handwork. And with her mother buried in the suds of the bathtub, there would be very little to do. She thought of the brazen young man in the elevator, and her cheeks flushed once again. She never would have considered going out with a stranger, but it was going to be awfully hard to think of some way to occupy her time in this luxurious prison.

"Why don't you call up some of your old friends, dear?" Elizabeth was asking as she moved toward the bathroom. "I saw a telephone right there by that green door to the left in the lobby."

My old friends, thought Christine. *You'd think after spending all those months in the city there'd be some old friends to call.* But she could think of no one. The truth was, her days and evenings in the city had been filled with Boyd, the boss's son, who had captured her heart. She could not even think of anyone from her old church youth group who might still be around and want to hear from her.

"I think I'll just rest," she told her mother. "I might even run down to the lobby and pick up the day's paper."

"A paper. That would be nice. I haven't read the news for who knows how long."

Christine picked up the room key and bounced it restlessly in her hand. It appeared that the paper was about her only entertainment possibility.

But the newspaper did little to lighten her evening. The headlines shouted the news of the conflict overseas. Photographs of smiling, uniformed young men and women, waving the victory sign, filled its pages. There was even a column of names of those who had "shipped out," sent off to England to be further prepared for the battle ahead. These who had such a short time ago been carefree young people with bright hopes for their tomorrow would perhaps in future lay in some foreign grave—if they had a grave at all.

Christine thought of Boyd. He had joined the air force. Was he still all right? Would she know if something happened to him? Would she be informed? No, likely not. She had no idea where he was, whether he was even alive. She found herself breathing another prayer on his behalf.

From the bathroom she could hear the sound of running water. Her mother was warming up the tub again. Christine tossed the paper on the nearby chair. The news it contained only served to depress her. She had already seen enough. With all her heart she prayed that Henry would not decide to go. Surely, surely, he had already made up his mind. He would not be leaving Amber and Danny.

But what about her? Had she a right to remain behind while other young people gave their lives in the cause of freedom? It didn't seem right. She had no more to live for than each of them. She was *ready* to die, should death be required. She knew she was prepared for eternity. Not because she was good, or favored, but because she had made peace with God. Yet she had no desire for life to be cut short.

She hated the war. Hated the selfishness, the greed that caused one country, one person, to feel superior to another. It wasn't right. Someone had to help stop this awful war.

But did she have to be involved? Was it her war? But neither was it theirs—the long list of volunteers who were the next wave of new recruits being "sent over."

Christine picked up the paper again and studied the smiling faces, searching carefully for one that might look like John or Wynn, their two young Indian friends. But many of the faces were a blur. She could not tell if there were any Cree among them.

She could hear her mother stirring in the next room. Evidently she had finished her long soak in the tub and would soon be coming out. Christine took a deep breath to help calm her churning feelings and questions. She hoped her face would not give her away. The evening would not be pleasant for either of them if she didn't get herself in hand.

She went to the window and swept back the heavy drapery. The night looked still and cold. Few hurried along the sidewalks. The scene brought no comfort. It was as barren and cold as her own heart felt right now. Somehow... somehow she had to find her way and some sense of what was taking place in the world. But for the moment, it made no sense at all.

CHAPTER FOUR

When they caught the train to Calgary the next morning, Christine thought she had never seen her mother so excited. Elizabeth chatted on and on about Jon and Mary and her time with them when she first came west to teach. She reminisced about each of their children—William, Sarah, Kathleen, and Lizbeth—recalling cute childish sayings and funny anecdotes. Christine wondered if her mother would be terribly disappointed to see her beloved children now as young adults.

As winter mornings go, it was a pleasant one with the sun reflected off the drifts of new snow, causing an intriguing play of shadows and light. Pristine fields stretched for miles, inviting someone—something—to be the first to string a thread of beaded track across the expanse. The distant hills rose in the crisp morning air, their tall pines like frosty sentinels against the blueness of the sky.

Christine found it hard to pull her eyes from the view rushing by the window. Even her mother's voice served not to distract her but rather to lay a background for the mood the scene evoked. The troubled thoughts about her future from the evening before had vanished. *Looking out on the world at hand, how could anyone not deem it good?* she wondered. *The vastness. The perfection. The beauty.* All spoke to her heart. She was glad to be alive. Glad to be a part of it. She felt her heart grow with joy. *This . . . this is what life is meant to be.*

A warning whistle sliced the morning air with a shrillness that was both melancholy and invasive, and they pulled into a small town. Christine leaned her head against the cool window and watched a scurry of activity. Horses stomped and blew great drafts of frosty air. Men called and pulled and heaved and loaded, their whiskers whitened by frozen breath. There were few women or children about. An occasional hand stirring aside a curtain was about as much indication that they, too, occupied the town. But Christine knew they were there. She saw it in the smoke that curled slowly up from the chimneys. In the small sleds leaning against woodsheds. In the snowmen in fenced yards and the brooms that stood beside the doors, inviting one to sweep the snow from boots and clothing before entering the kitchen.

She even thought she saw it in the scurrying of the men, for why else would they rush about in such inclement weather if not to provide for someone dear who shared the home?

The act of stopping, of observing, of moving on once again, was repeated throughout the day. Christine thought her mother paid little attention to the hustle and bustle, so was surprised when Elizabeth leaned forward, her entire face alight with excitement.

"Look," she cried. "We've reached Lacombe."

Christine had heard enough family history to know that Lacombe was the area where her mother had taught school. She had, on two occasions, visited her grandmother Delaney and her aunt, uncle, and cousins who still lived on the family farm outside the small town. Still, she was not prepared for Elizabeth's reaction.

"Oh, I wish we could stop. How I'd love to visit the school again. And the little teacherage. The dear little teacherage. I was so happy there."

Christine chuckled. "From what you've said before, I always thought you were quite miserable."

"Miserable?" The word seemed to shock Elizabeth.

"Yes. Wondering just who Dad was and if he cared at all for you."

To Christine's surprise, Elizabeth's cheeks flushed. "Well, he did keep me guessing," she admitted. "I thought he was Lydia's husband. It annoyed me because he . . . he seemed to . . . to pay some attention to me as well."

"But you wanted his attention."

"Not if he was a married man, I didn't." Elizabeth was emphatic.

"But you flirted—just a little bit." Christine couldn't help but prolong her mother's obvious discomfort a little further.

Elizabeth's face was now rosy with color. "I did not flirt. Well, I . . . I wished him to notice me . . . at first. But when I . . . when I thought he was married to Lydia, I certainly did nothing . . . nothing at all to draw his attention."

Elizabeth lowered her eyes and played with straightening her already smooth skirts. Christine could not hide her smile. She had never seen her mother so disturbed. She reached out and took Elizabeth's hand.

"Mama," she said, "if I'd seen him, I think I might not have been as honorable as you. I might have flirted—even if I had thought him a married man. He is so . . . so handsome . . . and in his uniform—"

"You would not have," declared Elizabeth, chin lifting. "I have raised you better than that."

She must have recognized the teasing in Christine's eyes

and realized she'd been baited. She gave the hand on hers a little shake. "You silly child," she said with a bit of a laugh. There was no chiding in her tone or words.

Christine leaned back in her seat again. "Tell me about it," she invited. "What was it like to live all alone in the teacherage in the country? Was it lonely?"

The flush left Elizabeth's face, and in its place Christine could see a thoughtfulness. A looking back on those years with fondness.

"Lonely? I suppose it was ... in a way ... at times. But no, not really. I missed my family. Dreadfully at first. I had never been away from home before. But ... but even so I always had this strange and ... and very real sense of peace that I was right where I should be. I'd sit in that lumpy old chair and sip my tea from my china cup at the end of the day and see those faces of the dear children I was privileged to teach and ..."

She stopped. A pensive look caused her eyes to shine with unshed tears. "I suppose they are all adults now with families ... and struggles ... and rewards of their own."

Christine nodded silently.

"But I ... I still like to think that somehow ... somehow I made a difference in their lives. The little I could teach them—the love that I could not help but show them—I like to think that it helped in some way to ... to shape them into whom they have become."

"I'm sure it did." The words were not more than a whisper.

They sat in silence for a few moments. Christine assumed her mother's full attention now was being given to the loading and unloading of goods on the platform of the Lacombe station, so she was surprised when Elizabeth spoke again.

"I've often thought of going back. Of inviting myself to a community picnic or a Christmas program. Some ...

some community event where I could see the most people in the shortest time. Someplace where they gather. But I've . . . I've never had the opportunity. Nor the courage."

"The courage?"

The train's whistle blew, long and loud. With a shudder that rattled the adjoined cars, the wheels began to turn once again. They were moving on.

"Things change so over the years. I guess . . . I guess I was afraid that I might . . . well . . . discover something that would damage my precious memories. Memories are so fragile, you know. Sometimes I feel they are best left undisturbed."

Christine thought about the words. At length she dared inquire, "Is that why you have never accepted Dad's invitation to take you back to the North?"

She saw Elizabeth's chin tremble. No answer was immediately forthcoming. When she turned to speak once again to her daughter, there were tears in her eyes.

"It was not easy making a home in the North. But I . . . I grew to love it. I suppose partly because I loved your father so. But I would never claim it was easy. At first I was so lonely. And a bit fearful too. The people were so . . . so different. I didn't know how to understand them . . . nor could I communicate with them.

"And then a strange thing happened. At least it seems rather strange when I look back on it. I began to make friends. Not just . . . just acquaintances but real, deep-down friends. I loved the people, Christine. The women. The darling children. And of course there was our precious Sammy. . . ." Elizabeth could not speak for a moment. Christine knew the story of the little Indian boy whom Elizabeth and Wynn had taken into their home and their hearts. And then, much later, his father had returned to claim him. . . . Christine had a lump in her throat as her mother wiped her eyes. But Elizabeth took a deep breath

51

and continued, "Those Indian women's lives were so . . . so hard. They endured so much.

"It was hard to leave them. I felt like . . . rather a traitor, actually. I was going back to many comforts. Many amenities. And they . . . they just had to stay where they were—*as they were*—and cope. I felt like I . . . deserted them."

"But you didn't."

Elizabeth raised her head. "When your father was injured and we thought we were going to lose him, something happened inside me. Before . . . before when I was afraid . . . or troubled, I always had him. He was my strength. My comfort. As long as I had that I could go on. But when I thought I might lose him, I realized that I had no strength of my own. Not really. If I lost him . . ."

Christine reached for her mother's hand again.

"The North nearly took him from me, Christine."

"But, Mama . . ."

"I was the one who pushed to get him back to a place that was more civilized. I don't think your father really wanted to come. He would have stayed right there, injured leg and all, and trekked the miles and camped in the cold and exposed himself to more half-crazy men. I . . . I think his heart is still in the North. If we went back—"

"I'm going back," Christine said impulsively. "I don't blame Dad for feeling that way. For loving it. He was . . . was needed there. Loved. The North was where he belonged."

She spoke with such vehemence that both of them were surprised.

"You are angry with me?" Elizabeth spoke softly.

Christine stirred on the worn plush seat, her sudden outburst now controlled.

"I'm not angry. Just . . . just a little upset, I guess. I love the North. You . . . you not only took Dad from it, but us . . . Henry and me too. It . . . it just doesn't seem fair."

Elizabeth toyed with the gloves in her lap. "I guess I did," she admitted. "And I'm sorry. But no . . . no, I'm not sorry. It was time for you to come out. Both of you. You needed to . . . to learn about the rest of the world. You needed to see things and hear things and—and grow up. And your father. He needed to be able to sleep in a bed at night. To have regular hours of work. To walk around without watching his back."

"Walk without 'watching his back'?" Christine was stirred to remonstrate, "But he was loved. And respected."

"By most. Yes. But there were always a few—those who had broken the law and been made to pay for it—who watched for opportunities to . . . well, let's just say your father had to be very vigilant when out on the trail."

"You never said—"

"Of course we didn't. We didn't want to frighten you. But it's a part of life for a Mountie."

"Does Henry . . . ?"

"If he has made enemies. Yes."

"But that's not fair."

"Life is never fair. The best one can hope for is to be given a chance."

Christine had much to ponder. It was the first time Elizabeth had really opened her heart to Christine—not simply as her daughter but now as a friend. In the past she had always been the protector. The guardian. Now she had exposed herself as vulnerable. Needy. Human. Christine was not sure how to respond.

She had one more question she had to ask. "Was . . . was Dad afraid?"

"Afraid? Sensibly so. Cautious. He worried at times that something might happen to him, and I'd—we'd be stranded with no way to get out of the North. No place to go. We talked of it. He . . . he kept a little stash of money—not much, but a little. He . . . he said if ever anything happened, I was to use it to find us a small house in some safe town. He said—"

But Christine did not wish to hear more. It was too much. All the morbid thoughts on such a brilliant day. She shivered and stopped her mother. "Look. There are tracks all across that field. Deer must have been playing tag or something."

Elizabeth chuckled. "We missed it," she lamented.

The spell was broken. Christine leaned her head back against the high seat and closed her eyes. Her emotions were still in turmoil. So much . . . so much had gone on in her family that she had been totally unaware of. So many battles fought and won—or lost. So many struggles with inner or outer conflicts. As a child she had assumed that grown-ups had everything neatly figured out. That they were in charge of their world. That there was nothing that troubled their sleep or caused them alarm. Now was she being told that there was never a place in the world free of worry or challenge? That was not what Christine was hoping to hear right now.

———

Both Jon and Mary met them at the Calgary station. "I just couldn't bear to wait at home," Mary exclaimed as she hugged first one, then the other. "It's been such a long time."

"Oh, it's so good to see you," responded Elizabeth, tears in her eyes. "I think of you all so often. And the children. How are the children?"

"Well," laughed Jonathan, "the children have children of their own now, as you know. They are quite adult. Quite, shall we say, independent—for which their mother and I are dreadfully thankful."

They all laughed.

"Oh, I want to see them. Each of them," enthused Elizabeth.

"And you shall. They are all coming to dinner tonight. Well, all, that is, except William. He and his family haven't been home since a year ago June. He took them all off to Winnipeg. Can't imagine it. But William loves it. He's an attorney, you know."

"Yes," murmured Elizabeth. "And a good one, too, I'm sure."

"Well, let's get you loaded up and off to our home," said Jonathan, lifting the two heavy suitcases. "We've plenty of time to talk in the comfort of the living room."

"I think the city has grown again," mused Elizabeth as she gazed out the car window.

"Grown. Growing. Every time you turn around, a new building is going up." Jonathan seemed very pleased and proud of his city.

"It's growing too fast, if you ask me," cut in Mary. "We can't keep up with things."

"We'll catch up," Jonathan replied comfortably.

Christine could not help but compare Calgary to the Edmonton she knew. It was true that Calgary was growing quickly. She noted several new buildings since the time she had spent with her uncle Jon and aunt Mary while taking her secretarial course. But if she had to choose in which of the two cities she would make her home, she was not sure which one it would be. They were very different—in both appearance and feel.

"You've changed the color of your house," Elizabeth exclaimed as they pulled up into the driveway.

"It was time for a change. It had the same blue-green trim for over thirty years."

"I liked it," said Elizabeth and quickly caught herself. "This looks nice too. Such a nice fresh color."

"It's very popular right now," spoke up Mary. "I suppose,

like everything else, it will need something new in the future. It no doubt will soon be dated. But for now…" She shrugged. "You know what they say, 'The only thing constant is change.' Or something like that."

Except in the North, thought Christine. *In the North things have stayed the same for generation after generation. And they will go on staying the same. That's what I like about the North. Well, at least, that's one thing I like.*

They shed their wraps and were shown to their rooms, then invited to the drawing room for a refreshing cup of tea and newly baked scones. There was no flickering fire in the fireplace.

"We really don't need it now, because the central heating's so effective," practical Mary explained. "We only light it if we feel sentimental. This is so much less messy."

But Christine missed the dancing of the flames and the crackle of burning logs. Central heating could not fill that need.

"So our Henry is getting married," Mary noted. "Wonderful. He stopped in and introduced us to his bride-to-be. She seems so sweet. And that little boy. Isn't he a darling? You must be thrilled, Elizabeth."

The talk swirled around Christine. It was clear the two women had much to talk about and were set to enjoy hours and hours of each other's company. Should she sit and listen or set her empty cup aside with a smile and retreat to her room? Or perhaps she could excuse herself with the need for some exercise. But she felt content. Lazy. At length she squirmed herself into a comfortable position in the overstuffed easy chair and settled down to enjoy the rise and fall of the familiar voices.

Dinner that evening was a rather boisterous affair. The table was crowded with family. Two high chairs and their tiny occupants pushed their way in between parents at either end of the table. The baby girl had been named Elizabeth in honor of her great-aunt, a fact that Elizabeth cooed and gushed over. The little boy, two months younger than his cousin, was named Matthew. He had large brown eyes and heavy lashes. Christine was sure she had never seen a prettier baby. Other little ones sat on stacked phone books or small orange crates placed on dining room chairs. The older two—seven and ten years old—were able to sit in adult-sized chairs. The boy was a little saucy but the girl quite sedate and grown-up in manner. Christine remembered them from her time spent in the city, but they had changed considerably over the years since she had left. They either did not remember her well or pretended they did not. At any rate, they responded only politely to her overtures.

The talk swirled around the table like incoming breakers, punctuated frequently by splashes of laughter. It was enough to make one feel dizzy. Elizabeth seemed to revel in it. Christine realized for the first time just how much her mother must have missed contact with family. No wonder her father had suggested she come early to *store up* once again.

At the thought of her father, Christine felt a twinge. Already she missed him. How was he faring all alone? Certainly he had no cause to go hungry with all the food her mother had left for him. Was he lonely? Did he miss the stir of his wife in the kitchen? The conversation before the open fire of an evening?

Perhaps he enjoys a few quiet moments to sort through his own thoughts, concluded Christine. *We all need quiet times now and then.*

But we all need communication as well, her silent soliloquy continued. *I would have never guessed that Mother felt some of the things she shared today. In the future, I must be more . . . more open, more prepared to listen. To sense her needs.*

It was certainly something new to think about.

CHAPTER FIVE

The next days passed pleasantly with much activity—some of it fun and some relating to wedding preparations. Actually, that was fun, too, Christine decided. Then the day arrived when Henry would come to Calgary and bring Christine back for the days leading up to his wedding. Her new suit was carefully folded in tissue and packed for the journey. She finally had chosen material of a soft navy, having come to the conclusion that the red serge of the Force was not an easy color to complement.

But she was pleased with the pattern they had found and most satisfied with her mother's skilled seamstress ability. The suit looked good on her. Even she could appreciate that fact. She did hope Amber would be equally happy with it.

One fact had dampened her visit to the bustling city. Everywhere she turned it seemed she saw young people in full uniform. Never had she imagined that so many of her country's youth were willing to go off to war. They seemed to swarm over the city, calling jovially from each street corner, congregating at bus stops, laughing and jostling at lunchroom counters.

"You'd think it was some adventurous lark, instead of a war that needs fighting," Christine heard one disgruntled matron exclaim to another. And it was true. The young men and women seemed to be celebrating rather than preparing for a dangerous undertaking that could cost them their lives. Perhaps they did have more sober moments when the enormity of what was at stake accosted them, but they appeared very careful not to let it show. *Maybe that's why,* Christine wondered. *They're trying to keep their spirits up to face what is ahead.*

The Sunday service had been another reminder. One of the young lads from the local congregation had just left for overseas. Serious, fervent prayer was offered up on behalf of the family who remained at home, forced to wait—and pray—hoping for his safe return.

"There are so many needs," the pastor informed them. "Not just overseas, but here at home as well. You ask how you might be involved? Seek ways. Look around you. There are hand projects. Gloves, socks, and toques are needed. Even sweaters can be knit and sent. You can make up CARE packages. Little bits of home for the young men and women over there.

"And the local clubs need help. Faith Church has started a drop-in center for the servicemen. We can help out. They serve coffee and cake and give the boys—and the young women, we have young women going too—a chance to gather and play games or just talk.

"And many of the businesses need employees. So many young men have gone that it is up to the womenfolk to take their places here on the home front. We need to keep our country productive if the war effort is to be successful. See what you can do to help—and prayerfully get involved."

Christine had not considered the involvement needed at

home. But it was true. There was much to be done here at home as well. Her prayers began to change from that time on. "Lord, show me how you want me to be involved. Don't let me jump in with my own plans. Show me, Lord."

Reminders. Everywhere were reminders. From signs asking the populace to buy war bonds, to posted lists in local papers, to news of advancing or retreating forces on each night's newscast, to uniformed youth on each city street. Every place Christine went she was confronted with the fact that Canada was at war.

At the sound of a car pulling up in the driveway, Christine hurried to answer the door. Elizabeth was right behind her.

Henry was unfolding his long legs from the car's interior. Christine was glad to see he was alone. She was looking forward to having him all to herself for one last time and hoped it was not selfishness on her part.

He walked toward them, heavy overcoat flapping in the afternoon wind, broad grin lighting his face. "Well, look at this. Two of my favorite women."

"Yes," Christine laughed. "We're glad we're still on your list!"

Elizabeth pushed past Christine to claim him first. She lifted her arms to pull him down so she could plant a kiss on his cheek. "How were the roads?" she asked as soon as he straightened.

"Fine. A few little drifts here and there—but nothing major. I had no trouble at all getting through."

She patted his cheek and backed away so Christine might also embrace Henry.

"Ready?" Henry asked.

"Everything is right here at the door," she informed him.

"Good."

"You're coming in, aren't you?" asked Elizabeth in

alarm. Surely he wasn't going to turn right around and head back was her unspoken meaning.

"For a few minutes. Not long. We need to get going before the roads—"

"I thought you said they were fine." Elizabeth held the door for Henry to enter.

"They were okay—but a wind is starting to come up. The roads can drift in quickly if it starts to blow."

Elizabeth frowned. "Perhaps you should get started, then." Her voice revealed her reluctance. She hated to let them go.

Henry must have sensed her discomfort and changed course. He removed the heavy overcoat and hung it in the closet. "Thought Aunt Mary might have one of her good cups of coffee ready."

"She has just rushed to the phone to call Jonathan. He said to let him know the minute you arrived. He's coming right home."

"Oh, he shouldn't do that. I can't stay long."

"He said a little break will do him good."

Henry nodded. "So how has your time in the city been?" he asked.

"Delightful," exclaimed Elizabeth. "I've soaked in the tub every night."

Henry laughed loudly. "You come to the bustling city of Calgary and sit in the tub?" But his teasing elicited no response from his mother except a little wave of her hand at him.

"And you?" He turned to Christine. "Did you get a chance at the tub?"

"Well, I haven't spent as much time in there as Mother, but yes, I've had my turn."

When Mary burst through the door, Henry rose to greet her. "Your uncle Jon will be right home. It only takes him a minute. My—I think you get taller every time I see you. I have to stand on tiptoe just to reach for a hug."

Henry wrapped long arms about his aunt and gave her a warm embrace. "It's awfully good to see you, Aunt Mary."

"I have enjoyed Christine so much. We've had such fun together. And I'm so glad to have this special time with your mother. We've had so much to talk about. I just wish there weren't so many miles separating us. It really doesn't seem fair that our country is so big. Now sit. I've got Lucy bringing the coffee. I know you'll be in a hurry to get back before dark. Wish we could keep you here for a few days, but I know that's impossible.

"How are Amber and Danny?" Mary rushed on. "Is she getting *new-bride's nerves* yet? It's getting awfully close, isn't it? Are things going smoothly with the plans? I'd love to help. Wish I was closer. I said to Jon that I'd just love to bake the wedding cake or help with the decorations. Does Amber like that sort of thing? Maybe she doesn't even need help. She certainly looks like she has things together. What about Danny? Is he excited about having a new daddy?"

Henry hardly knew which question to answer, so he merely nodded his head and let his aunt keep talking.

Mary eventually stopped abruptly when Lucy arrived with a tray bearing a steaming coffeepot and a number of cups. The tray also held a plate of beef sandwiches and a lemon sponge cake.

"I thought you might be a bit hungry after your long drive. I don't want you to go away without something in your stomachs."

"It looks and smells delicious, Aunt Mary."

"We'll not wait for Jonathan. He never eats between meals. He'll just want coffee." And the sandwiches were passed first to Henry and then to Christine.

"You'd better eat up," Henry warned her. "Who knows when you'll get the chance again? Not many restaurants between here and my place. And not much in my cupboards either."

Christine followed his advice. They were still enjoying the repast when Jonathan arrived. After hearty greetings, he accepted the cup of black coffee from his wife and settled into the chair next to Henry.

For the next few moments it was man-talk that flowed in the parlor. Christine noted Henry's eyes lifting to the face of the grandfather clock now and then. The hands were busily ticking away the minutes, and Christine knew Henry was anxious about the time. She decided to aid him in the matter.

"I'll just get my wraps from the bedroom and join you in the hall."

He nodded, his eyes thanking her for her understanding.

There was the usual flurry of last-minute cautions and embraces. And then they were in the car and moving off through the city streets toward the open highway. Henry looked intent on getting out of the city and onto the highway, so it was several minutes before either of them spoke.

"How has your visit been?" asked Henry finally.

"Good. We bought the material and Mother did a great job of sewing the suit."

"Mother always does."

Christine nodded. "I hope Amber likes our choice."

"Amber will love it."

"Oh, so we speak for her now, do we?" teased Christine.

Henry grinned. "You know what Scripture says. 'They shall become one.'"

"But you're not one yet."

"No—not yet. It seems every day drags just a little bit more. I never knew time could pass so slowly," Henry groaned.

Christine knew he was teasing, but she couldn't keep

from casting him a sideways glance. "So you haven't had second thoughts?"

"Every day I am more convinced."

She nodded. "That's good."

"What about you?" he asked after a moment's silence. "Have you had any second thoughts?"

"About Boyd, you mean? No. No second thoughts. It was the only thing I could do. But . . . but I do worry at times. I wonder. If . . . if I had held to my Christian standards, could I have done more to introduce him to Christ? He's in the air force, you know. I sometimes think how awful it would be if his plane was shot down—with him not having made peace with God."

Henry nodded, his face serious.

"There are a lot of them in that circumstance, I'm afraid. Marching off to war with no hope should they die in the trenches. It's scary."

"Calgary was full of them. Everywhere you looked—uniforms."

"I know. I saw them when I drove in."

The wind had indeed picked up. Snow scurried across the road ahead of them in wavy shivers. Henry held the wheel firmly to keep the car headed straight.

"Have you—did you ever think about—I mean, did you ever have any thoughts about enlisting?" Christine finally found courage to ask.

"Many thoughts. And doubts. And struggles."

"You did?"

"I did. I don't remember wrestling in prayer as much over any other matter."

Christine could feel her throat constrict. "Have you decided? You're not going—are you?"

"I planned to. I even drove in to headquarters to hand in my resignation to the Force. But I was talked out of it."

"Talked out of it? Amber?"

"No—not Amber. We had talked it over—many times, actually—and she knew it had to be my decision. No, it was my superiors. They said there are two jobs to be done in wartime. Some need to go. But there is also a job that needs to continue being done at home—to keep stability. To hold things together so those who have gone will have something to come back to. We need a strong, secure base. Our boys need that."

Christine let her breath out slowly. Henry would not be going off to war.

"So you are—you feel at peace about it all now?"

"I do. Oh, it wasn't just the conversations. It was a scripture I read when I was searching for the answer. It seemed to speak to me directly. It talked about 'staying by the stuff.' I realized that was an important part of the job too. It's not a case of copping out. Not when you take your duties seriously."

"Amber must be relieved."

Henry smiled. "She is. But she would have let me go if it had turned out that way. She said that God must govern my life—not a wife."

Christine remained silent. That was something else to think about.

———

They were thankful to climb from the car in front of Henry's small house. The roads had gotten increasingly difficult. The last few miles of drifts caused concern, though Henry tried not to let on. He only had to get out the shovel once, but Christine felt that was once too often.

The first thing Henry did was to phone Amber. "We're here—safe and sound. No . . . no, they weren't too bad. A little tricky in spots. Is Danny sleeping? Give him a kiss for me. I'll see you in the morning. I'll drop by the shop. And

I'll bring Christine over later. Okay. Right. Sleep tight. Me too."

Christine wondered what else would have been said had she not been waiting, suitcase in hand.

"She says to give you her love." Henry turned from the phone and took the suitcase from Christine. "Right this way."

"But this is your room," Christine objected.

"I moved my stuff into the lean-to," he said matter-of-factly.

"But it'll be cold."

"No, I put in a little heater. It gets too hot at times." Christine did not argue further.

"Want something to eat?"

"I ate loads of Aunt Mary's sandwiches. I think I'll just crawl in."

"Me too. It's been a long day. Anything you need, just holler."

Henry was poking around in the potbellied stove. "Good. There's still a bit of fire. I just have to bank it for the night or we'll both be icicles in the morning."

"Doesn't the town have gas heat?"

"The town does. I don't."

Christine stifled a yawn. "You'll call me?"

"For breakfast. Promise."

"Good night, then."

Christine moved to go, still yawning.

"Chrissy," Henry called after her.

She turned slowly.

"It's good to have you. I've looked forward to this."

"Me too," she answered with a smile. She had never meant anything more sincerely.

They shared a simple breakfast together. Then Henry rose and began to gather up his heavy coat and gloves. "I need to get down to the office. You'll be okay?"

Christine nodded. "And you need to stop by the barbershop," she teased him. "Don't forget."

Henry grinned. "I'm not likely to forget."

"Is there anything you'd like me to do?"

"Nothing special. We're going over to Amber's for supper tonight. We'll talk things over then. I thought you might like to walk over to the office about noon, and we'll go for lunch at the café."

"The café? That sounds like fun."

"Well—it all depends how heavy Jessie's gone on the spice can today."

Henry flipped on his Stetson and turned to go.

"I'll see you later, then," called Christine as the door closed on his tall form.

If he weren't my brother, I might fall for him, she mused with a smile. He was so good-looking in his uniform.

Christine busied herself washing up the breakfast dishes. There really wasn't much in Henry's small home that needed attention. He kept things remarkably orderly and clean for a bachelor. Christine did find a recent magazine she had not previously seen and loafed away the morning with some reading.

She kept one eye on the clock. At fifteen to twelve she wrapped up and took to the street. Henry had given careful directions to the office, only a few blocks away. Sure enough, the small building with its sign, *Royal Canadian Mounted Police*, soon came into sight. She had been familiar with such stations all her life, so she felt no trepidation as she pushed the door open and stepped inside. Her eyes roamed quickly over the interior. It was much like the offices her father had occupied—yet different in some way.

Three desks were scattered about the room. Only one

was occupied—and that not by Henry. She looked beyond, where two doors led off the main room.

"You Christine?" a male voice asked as the young man in uniform stood to his feet.

Her glance turned back to him. He was not as tall as Henry and a bit stockier. His hair was very dark and his eyes even more so. At the moment they seemed a bit puzzled.

Christine nodded.

"Henry said *kid* sister," he muttered half under his breath.

Christine nodded again. She finally found her tongue. "Where *is* Henry?"

"Well, he got called out—unexpectedly."

"Out? To where?"

"Some farmer had him a problem. Henry didn't explain. Just said he'd be back as soon as he could."

Christine shifted slightly, wondering what she should do next.

"Was... was I supposed to wait for him here?" she asked, feeling awkward and childish.

The young Mountie's face reddened. "Well—that wasn't really the plan. I mean..." He looked down at his highly polished boots. "Henry said, 'My kid sister's coming. I told her I'd take her to the café. If I'm not back in time, will you take her on over?' I said, 'Sure.'"

"I... I see," stammered Christine.

"So if you don't mind, I'd like to keep the agreement with my boss."

He was still blushing.

"You must have work to do."

"A man has to eat."

"Yes... I guess so," Christine said, feeling a bit annoyed with Henry for putting them both in this awkward predicament.

The man reached for his Stetson. "So...?" he asked.

Christine managed a smile. "So . . ." she responded. "Let's go eat."

He seemed much relieved. "I have to warn you," he said as he held the door for her, "Jessie likes the spices."

"So I've been told."

"Henry already warn you?"

Christine nodded, then began to laugh. "I consider myself thoroughly warned. I'll depend on you to steer me through the menu."

"Well—you can have peppered scrambled eggs or peppered stew or super-peppered chili. Take your pick."

Christine laughed more heartily, and the young officer joined in.

CHAPTER SIX

They were halfway through the meal when Henry made his appearance. He didn't even bother with an apology. Christine was feeling more relaxed as she chatted with her lunch partner. She did, however, give Henry a look of relief.

"So what's for lunch?" he asked as he took the chair next to her. With a quick glance at the menu, then a look at Christine's toast and tea, he asked, "Is that all you're eating?"

Christine nodded, then lowered her voice. "With double warning about spice, I decided to play it safe."

"It's not that bad," he whispered behind the menu. "What are you having, Laray?"

"Laray?" Christine raised an eyebrow.

"You haven't met?"

"Oh yes. We've met. I just haven't been told who it is I've met."

Laray flushed. "Sorry," he stammered. "I just never thought—"

But Christine waved his apology aside. "It's okay. I should have known. You're the one who took on the bear."

"Actually—it was the bear's idea. I gladly would have passed up the experience."

Christine turned sober. "How is your arm?"

"Gets a little better all the time. Soon the fellas won't be able to use it as an excuse to make me do all the office paper work while they cruise around in the squad cars."

Henry laughed.

"You decided?" asked a young waitress, setting a cup of coffee in front of Henry.

"I'll have what he's having." Henry nodded toward Laray and handed the menu back to the girl. "What are you having?" he asked Laray when she was out of earshot.

"The lasagna."

"Any good?"

"Yeah, if you like spice."

Henry took a swallow of coffee. "One thing you've got to say for Jessie," he said as he put down the cup. "She's sure not stingy with the coffee beans."

Laray nodded. "But I sometimes wonder just how long she uses the same ol' ones."

"Stop it, you two," Christine said, giving Henry a playful kick under the table.

"I forgot," said Henry. "We'd best mind our manners. There's a lady present."

Laray shot him a glance. "You told me she was your kid sister."

"She is. My kid sister."

"She's hardly a kid."

"I also told you she was to be Amber's maid of honor—didn't I?"

Laray shook his head. "I don't recall anything being said about the maid of honor."

"Well, then—meet the maid of honor."

At Laray's look of surprise, Christine remembered that he was the one to be Henry's best man. It seemed they would be seeing more of one another.

For a moment Laray appeared at a loss for words. He flushed slightly, then recovered with a wisecrack. "At least I'll be able to escort you on my good arm."

Christine felt her own face flushing.

"Hey," said Henry as though suddenly thinking of something. "We're having supper with Amber tonight to go over wedding plans. How about joining us, Laray?"

Laray shifted his feet. "I think you'd better check that out with the little lady first."

"Amber won't mind. I'll give her a call as soon as I get back to the office."

"I wasn't talking about Amber," mumbled Laray, giving Christine a sideways glance.

Henry turned to Christine, a frown creasing his forehead. It was clear he thought of no reason for her to object.

"Fine," she said with a lift of her shoulders. "If it's okay with Amber, it sounds fine with me."

———————

Christine walked over to Amber's barbershop that afternoon to offer to help with the supper preparations. On the way to Amber's home, they stopped at her folks to pick up Danny. He lost little time in expressing his feelings over the coming marriage.

"Mama says you will be my new auntie," he said, skipping alongside Christine.

"That's right."

"And I get another grandpa and grandma too."

"You do."

"Did you know my dad got dead?"

She hardly knew how to respond. Apparently Amber had thought it important to tell Danny the truth about his father's logging accident and death. Christine nodded.

"I don't remember him ... but if he was still alive, he'd remember me."

"I'm sure he would."

"But he's not—so I'm gonna get a new dad."

"Yes, I know."

"He's real nice. Mom and I like him. Lots. That's why we're gonna marry him. I'm gonna be ring—ring what, Mom?" He stopped abruptly in front of his mother.

"Ring bearer."

"Ring bear," he repeated, picking up the pace again. "That's a funny name. It just means I carry a ring on a pillow. Ring bear. I saw a bear one time. It was sorta black and sorta brown. It ran into the trees. Mom said it was scared. I couldn't hurt a bear. It's too big."

Christine couldn't help but smile. She wondered if Danny was always as excited and talkative, or if the coming wedding was making him extra energetic.

"Did you know there's a war someplace? They're fighting over there. With real guns. Teacher showed us on the map."

Oh my, thought Christine. *Why would a teacher inflict that news on her students? Little children shouldn't have to face such tragedies. . . .*

"Two people have gone from here," Danny was explaining, gesturing with his hands. "Sam somebody and—and I don't know his name. They were cowboys, but they have gone to the war. But they aren't over in that place yet. They still have to learn how to be soldiers. To shoot their guns and things. When they learn all that stuff—then they will go to war."

Christine inwardly cringed. Was there no way to get away from it? Did even the young have to be dragged into it? It didn't seem right that a child had to learn so much about the wickedness of war at such a young age.

Amber must have been thinking the same thoughts.

"Mrs. Wilbur told you all this?"

"Na-uh," he said shaking his head. "Tommy did. Tommy told all us kids about it. Rebecca was so scared she started to cry. I think she thought the war was going to come here, so Mrs. Wilbur showed us on the map. It's a long, long way away. Even over the ocean. But Rebecca says she'll have bad dreams anyway. She always has bad dreams about something. Snakes and mean cats and even spiders. She always has bad dreams."

Christine and Amber exchanged bemused glances over Danny's head. At least it was a relief to know it wasn't the schoolteacher who was filling little heads with scary stories.

"What do you think we should have for supper?" Amber asked. Christine recognized the diversion. "We're having guests, you remember."

"Pancakes," cried Danny clapping his hands.

"I'm not sure our guests would appreciate pancakes for supper. They're better for breakfast."

Danny looked surprised.

"I think they would rather have something more . . . more meat and potatoes."

"Would you?" Danny turned a quizzical face to Christine. She hated to be the one to deny him his pancakes.

"I think pancakes are just fine. But I agree with your mother. Sometimes working men do like their meat and potatoes."

He looked up at his mother. "Then if we need meat, let's have fried fish."

"I'm afraid I don't have any fish right now."

"What do you have?"

"Chicken."

"Okay. We'll have fried chicken," he agreed, but less than enthusiastically.

The three entered Amber's neat kitchen and deposited bags of groceries they had picked up on the way. Danny began to unload the contents. "Hey," he called. "This is good." He waved a package of marshmallows.

"Now, don't you get into that. I need it for the dessert I'm making," cautioned his mother.

"Not even one?"

"Not even one."

Danny started to the cupboard with the package.

"No need to put it away. I'm going to use it as soon as I change my dress and wash my hands. Why don't you get yourself a cookie and some milk, then you can go play with your truck."

"Do I need to change my clothes too?"

"Please."

"I'll change first—then get the cookies."

"Cookie," corrected Amber.

Danny ran off to change.

Chatting as they worked, the two cooks in the kitchen did not take long to have the meal well under way. Christine felt she finally would have the sister she had always longed for. She wished their lives were not to be lived so many miles apart.

"You did meet Laray?" Amber wondered.

"I did. Henry invited me to the café for lunch, but he stood me up. Guess Laray drew the short straw."

"He's a great guy. Henry really likes him."

"He seems nice enough."

"It was such a shame—that accident with the bear. But he's coming along really well. Henry says he has almost all the movement back in his arm again. Not quite the strength, but that'll come."

Amber tasted the gravy, nodding her approval. "Not even lumps," she said with satisfaction.

The doorbell rang, and Danny rushed through the house. "It's your friend, Mom," he called.

Amber smiled. "It has been a bit of a problem deciding

what Danny should call Henry until after the big day. We didn't think 'Dad' was appropriate yet. And we didn't want Henry—but anything else sounds so formal."

"Well, it won't be long now until 'Dad' will be just right." Christine smiled at the thought of her brother as a father.

"Eight days. Can you believe it? Only eight days."

Danny led Henry in by the hand. "He brought the other guy too, Mom," he announced with a wave toward Laray.

"Come right in, 'other guy,' " invited Amber with a laugh. "We are just dishing up."

"I can't wait," said Henry taking a deep breath.

"Go ahead and be seated. It's going to be a little tight around our small table—but we'll manage. Laray, you can just take one of those back chairs."

Laray thanked his hostess and slid in as directed.

All gathered around the table, and Laray was asked to say the grace. The food and the laughter and banter passed easily around the table. Even Danny was outtalked.

Christine could not remember having such a relaxed, fun evening for a very long time. After Danny was tucked in bed, the four began serious talk about wedding details. Amber pulled out a sheet of paper and drew little diagrams with stick men as she explained how she wished the entrance to the altar area to be arranged.

"Dad will not be giving me away this time. He's already done that. He and Mom will be seated here before the ceremony begins." She turned her eyes to Henry. "You and the minister will come in from the study door, here."

He nodded, looking serious, Christine thought.

"Then Laray and Christine will walk in from the back—here."

"You mean I won't have him to prop me up?" Henry's little quip seemed to relax him a bit.

"I thought it would be nice if they'd walk in together."

Henry conceded.

"Then Danny and I will walk in."

"Together?"

"He might do something—well, silly, if he comes in alone. Besides, I might need him to hold my hand."

"That's cute," said Christine.

"Truthfully, I do want him with me. It's just . . . well . . . things will change . . . after. It's been just Danny and me for so long. One last time—the two of us. Do you mind?"

"Not at all," Henry quickly assured her. He reached out and took her hand. Christine saw Amber's fingers curl tightly about Henry's. "From then on—it's the three of us," she promised.

Amber pulled out another list. "Here's where I'm at. The organist—Mrs. Claire. The soloist—Clarice has agreed to sing the two songs we've picked, Henry. The decorations—Mrs. Boone will do them, but she'd like to have some help."

"I'll do that," volunteered Christine.

"Would you? Thank you. It will really free up my day if you could help her. The cake—Mrs. Dickus is providing that."

"Sounds like you have things pretty well worked out." Henry sounded impressed.

"There's lots to do yet," Amber sighed.

"I'll be glad to help in any way I can," Christine offered. "That is what I'm here for."

"I'm so thankful for another pair of hands—or another head," she added with a chuckle. "The reception will be in the church hall. It'll be a rather small affair, but there is the setting up and the arranging of the cake and the decorations and all. We'll move the flowers from the sanctuary, but someone will need to be in charge of getting that done."

"I can do that," said Laray. Then with a quick look to Henry, "Okay? You'll not be needing me then, will you?"

"Not once the photographer is done."

"It should work," Amber said, chewing on the end of her pencil. "We aren't having too many pictures taken."

On they went through the list, ticking off items one by one. By the time they had finished it was after ten. Christine was feeling very glad she had come early to help. She made her own list of the duties she had volunteered to carry through. Laray asked her to write down his jobs as well. Then Amber put on fresh coffee and served another helping of dessert, and they talked of other things.

It was a cold, crisp evening when they bid one another good night on the doorstep. Henry had not brought the car, so the three walked through the darkness together, linking arms in order to save space on the narrow sidewalk.

"Look at those stars tonight," Henry observed. "I've never seen them so bright."

"Maybe you see them with different eyesight these days," teased Laray. "They look just the same to me."

"I miss the northern lights. Do you ever see them this far south?" asked Christine.

"I've not," answered Henry.

"I've never seen them—ever," put in Laray.

"Never?" Christine was incredulous.

"Never."

"Oh, you've no idea. They are so . . . so spectacular. So beautiful. And they dance and flit across the sky—all colors. You can hear them swish. You feel like you could just reach out and . . . and grab a handful of the magic, they are so close."

"You sound like you're in love too," Henry joked.

They all laughed, then Laray said seriously, "I'd like to see them."

"Oh, you should."

"Now, don't get off on that, Sis," Henry chided softly. "When she gets started on the North and its many splendors, she gets all dreamy," he warned Laray.

"I can't help it," admitted Christine. "I love it."

They reached the corner where they would part ways. Laray seemed a bit reluctant to take his leave. "See you. Tomorrow?" he said.

Henry did not answer.

"Are you brave enough to try Jessie's again?"

This time it was obvious that Laray was speaking to Christine.

"I plan to get Henry's lunch at home tomorrow," she answered. "I know where to shop for groceries now," she explained.

"Lucky Henry," said Laray, kicking at a hunk of snow by the roadside.

With another good-night they moved off. It was late, and morning duties started early. Tomorrow would be a new day.

———

As she had planned, Christine had Henry's lunch ready at twelve o'clock sharp. He phoned five minutes later to say he was sorry, but he would be late. He'd had a call from a rancher and had to go check it out.

"Will it keep?" he asked her of the meal.

She was disappointed. She had worked the entire morning to prepare some of Henry's favorite things. "Well, I can warm it up again tomorrow. But it won't be as good as it would be today."

"Tell you what—I'll send Laray over. He'd love a home-cooked meal."

"Henry, you can't do that. How will it look to the . . . the townspeople?"

"Oh," said Henry. Just "Oh."

"Well, then, why don't you pack it up and bring it on down to the office?"

"Pack it up? It wouldn't stay hot two minutes."

"Then Laray can pick up Amber, and you can have them both over. That'd look all right, wouldn't it?"

"It's okay. We can eat it tomorrow."

"No. No . . . you've worked hard." Henry seemed to be thinking. "Tell you what. I'll stop at home on my way out of town. I'll bring Laray with me."

There was nothing to be done but to set another plate. Christine hoped she had prepared enough. She hadn't counted on feeding two hungry men.

But Henry hardly stopped at home long enough to eat. He hurriedly downed some of her fried potatoes and a small piece of meatloaf, then shoved another slice between two biscuits, wrapped it in a napkin, and refilled his coffee cup. "I've got to run." And he was gone.

"I'm sorry," began Christine as the door closed behind Henry. "I didn't know . . ."

"Guess his loss is my gain," Laray said comfortably. "We get used to eating on the run like that. Don't worry about Henry. More than he usually gets. And lots better tasting too."

Christine poured more coffee and passed the meatloaf again. "I hope you have time to at least chew it," she quipped.

Laray grinned as he took a bite.

"You're a very good cook," he said a while later as he reached for his Stetson. "Let's see. Who can I set up to call Henry tomorrow?"

Christine managed to laugh. "Henry is off tomorrow. He and Amber are driving into Lethbridge for some shopping. I'm going to look after Danny for them."

"'Fraid I'm on duty. All day. Wish I could help you out with Danny."

"He's no problem."

"Wish I could help you out just the same." He gave Christine another grin, a little lopsided this time. She felt her cheeks growing warm.

"Thanks for the lunch. Much better than Jessie's. Maybe you should start up a restaurant in the town. Give her a little competition."

Christine laughed. "Not me. No, sir. Even lots of spice couldn't hide my failures."

"It was delicious."

"Guess I lucked out."

"That's not what I'm thinkin'. I'm the one who lucked out."

Laray placed his Stetson on his dark hair, gave Christine another grin, and left.

After he had gone, she stood pondering the exchange. Just what had he meant? Was he flirting with her? Could he possibly think it had been her idea that he come for lunch? She was going to have a serious talk with her brother.

CHAPTER SEVEN

Christine was surprised at how busy the next week was. Besides trying to cook and do a bit of light housework for Henry, she spent many hours looking after Danny while Amber arranged last-minute details, and further hours ticking off assignments from her own to-do list. Christmas Eve, the date of the wedding, would fall on a Friday night. On Thursday Elizabeth and Wynn arrived, along with Jonathan and Mary. This meant additional people for meals and visits, even though arrangements had been made for the two couples to stay with Amber's folks.

Though Henry appeared to stay remarkably calm, Amber was beginning to get the jitters. Danny was doing jigs across the kitchen floor where others were making preparations for the reception.

"Danny, you must get out from underfoot," scolded Amber. "I'm afraid someone will run into you with something hot."

"I'm gonna get a dad—pretty quick," he sang out, moving to a corner but not leaving the kitchen.

The weather had cooperated better than any of them

had dared to hope. Though the winter temperatures meant one did not stay outside for more than a few minutes at a time, no more heavy storms with blowing snow had swept again across the open prairie. *Thank you, Lord,* Christine whispered as she went about her work.

She'd had her little talk with Henry and made herself quite clear. She did not wish to be thrust into repeated contact with Laray. True, he seemed like a fine young man, but she was far from ready for any kind of new relationship. Later she wondered if Henry had spoken with Laray. The young Mountie was conspicuously absent from then on. Christine almost regretted her hasty decision. She did hope she'd done nothing to hurt him. What if he thought her hesitancy was related to the injury of his arm? He gave little hints that he was conscious of the fact he no longer was the man he had been.

But Christine had little time to worry about it. Every waking moment was given to getting ready for the wedding. She'd had no idea that weddings, even rather simple ones, took so much time and preparation.

Once Elizabeth was on the scene, she, with Mary in tow, hurried about doing this and getting involved in that. Christine realized her mother was truly trying to help and to feel a part of it all, but in reality it made things more difficult. The carefully prepared lists of duties were continually being disrupted and changed. No one had the courage or insensitivity to ask the two enthusiastic women to please refrain from being so helpful.

Friday morning dawned bright and cold. So cold that Christine had to shelter her face as she quickly walked the short distance to Amber's house. She didn't remember even the North being so frigid. But then, she had been more prepared for the cold in the North. Fur-trimmed parkas were quite different from filmy squares of thin cotton over one's head.

Somehow they made it through the day with most things falling into place quite nicely. Henry, who was to pick up the flowers from Lethbridge, did wonder if they would freeze before he got them home. Laray, who had accompanied him, ended up cradling Amber's bouquet in his arms all the way back. The car heater was barely able to keep the interior of the motor vehicle above freezing.

The wedding was set for five o'clock—the earliest hour that light from the candles would be effective. The wedding guests would be ushered to the church hall immediately after for the reception that was to follow. While they were being settled, photographs would be taken of the bridal party before the altar. Then, all going well, the wedding supper would proceed.

It would undoubtedly be late when they finished the short program and the opening of gifts. Henry had decided not to risk taking to the roads on their honeymoon at such a late hour. Instead, he made arrangements with a local rancher to borrow a small cabin tucked away in the hills just west of town.

Laray knew of the location. It was his duty to lay a fire so the place would be nice and warm by the time Henry and his new bride arrived. Christine had been told of the plan, though she had not seen the cabin. It sounded wonderfully romantic to her. A cozy cabin in the woods with an open fireplace and light by candles. Henry had even arranged to have his bearskin rug spread out before the fire.

Christine's thoughts once again went to Boyd. She had loved him. The thought of her wrong choice still made her heart ache, even though she no longer felt drawn to the man. He had so much anger and arrogance buried deep within his soul. She did pray that he would one day soon give himself to God.

"Do you, Amber, take Henry . . ."

The familiar words of the service registered in Christine's mind and heart. She stood with Amber, who looked lovely in her wedding suit, holding her flower bouquet. Christine glanced beyond to Henry, handsome and stalwart in his officer's uniform. She blinked back tears, surprised at her own emotions, as she realized he now belonged to the woman beside him. She heard Amber's trembling yet firm response, "I do."

Then came Danny's loud whisper, "Is he my dad now?"

Laray's "shh" was drowned out by the ripple of laughter across the congregation. "Soon," Christine heard Laray whisper. Danny wiggled one foot, shod in a brand-new pair of black loafers, and plucked at the ribbon holding the rings on the pillow. Christine feared he'd somehow manage to pull them off. She sent a wordless message to Laray, who reached down and took Danny's restless fingers in his own. Christine sent another message of appreciation.

When the couple exchanged rings, Christine was relieved that the two small gold circlets had safely been transferred from Danny's small cushion and onto the appropriate fingers.

The ceremony continued. ". . . I now pronounce you man and wife," she eventually heard the minister say.

"Now?" asked Danny, and Laray nodded.

Danny's ring pillow was tossed into the air along with a triumphant whoop, then he flung his arms around Henry's legs. There were tears in more than just Henry's eyes as he lifted the little boy up. The groom's kiss of his new bride turned out to be a three-way event. Christine could hardly see through her own tears. She was very glad she had remembered to tuck a hankie in her bouquet. When she managed to recover, she discovered that somehow in all of the emotion of the moment, she was standing with her hand firmly held by Laray. Had she reached for him? Had he seen her tears and offered support? She had no idea how it had happened. Her cheeks burned with embarrassment. How was she to escape without making a scene? She need not have worried. Almost immediately she felt Laray's fingers gently release hers.

Danny, Henry, and Amber finally finished their hugs and returned to the decorum fitting a wedding ceremony. But Danny's eyes sparkled as Henry put him on his feet and he turned to Laray. Before Laray's finger could even go to his lips in warning, Danny announced proudly, "He's really my dad now."

Laray nodded while the minister said, "Ladies and gentlemen, may I introduce Sergeant and Mrs. Henry Delaney—and their son, Danny."

Warm and lengthy applause followed the wedding party out the door.

———

The long day was winding down. Christine, now changed from her new wedding suit to a simple skirt and sweater, heels exchanged for a pair of knitted slippers, pushed a tendril of hair behind her ear and rolled another length of crepe-paper streamer.

"Tired?" Laray was able to offer his sympathy in the one word.

"Exhausted," she replied, but she did manage the hint of a smile.

"We're almost done."

She nodded.

"Why don't you sit and I'll finish?"

"I'm fine."

"Thought maybe we could grab a cup of coffee when we're done. Relax a bit."

"Where? Even Jessie won't be open on Christmas Eve."

Laray nodded. "Maybe we'll have to make our own."

"Where?" Christine couldn't cover her surprise at the suggestion.

Laray seemed to think it over, but when he answered her, Christine wondered if he hadn't thought it through already.

"You're going from here to take care of Danny?"

"Right. Mom and Dad took him home to bed, but I said I'd take over."

"Maybe we can use Amber's kitchen."

Before Christine could voice an objection, he continued in a teasing manner, "Not much I can do, but I sure make a mean cup of coffee."

Christine couldn't help but laugh. "Okay. A cup of coffee. Maybe Mom and Dad will be ready for one too."

If that wasn't really what Laray had in mind, he did not say so.

Shortly Christine was placing the last of the decorations in their boxes. "Finally. Thanks so much for your help. I'd have been here till midnight if you hadn't."

"I hate to tell you this—but it's almost midnight now."

Christine glanced at her watch. "It is. No wonder I'm so tired. Now we have to load this stuff."

"Why don't we just stack it here? I'll pick it all up in the morning."

"Don't you have to work?"

"Rogers is on early shift tomorrow. I take over in the afternoon."

Christine nodded, thankful to call it a day. She pulled off her slippers and slipped into her boots. "If you want to stop by and pick me up, I'll help," she suggested.

She didn't miss the light in Laray's eyes. "I'll do that."

"Providing, of course, it's not too early."

"How early is too early?"

"Noon," she laughed.

"What about Danny?"

"Henry's coming back for Danny to take him out to the cabin. They'll have their first Christmas morning together."

"Hey—that's great. That brother of yours thinks of everything. Does Danny know?"

"We didn't dare tell him. Thought he'd never sleep if he was looking forward to that. Or he might have insisted in going with them tonight."

Laray reached for Christine's coat and helped her into it. When they left the church, Christine was surprised to discover that warmer air had replaced the extreme cold, and a light snow had begun to fall. She lifted her face toward the heavens and let the large, fluffy flakes cool her warm cheeks. "It's beautiful," she whispered. "Just what Christmas Eve should be."

Laray cleared his throat. "Speaking of beautiful . . ." He hesitated. "You looked pretty good today."

Christine's head came around. She did hope he wasn't going to make any silly speeches, but he said nothing more. "Thank you," she murmured in response to the compliment. After all, "pretty good" was not so hard to accept.

After the short drive to Amber's house, they saw a light glowing from the front window. Christine could see her mother in an easy chair, head leaned back in rest. Christine smiled. She looked so nice in her gray suit spruced up with a new blouse of pale blue silk. She was glad her father had talked her into purchasing it.

Christine was about to open the front door when she felt Laray's restraining hand on her own. He was standing close—very close. It made her feel uneasy. He held out his pocket watch, which she could barely read in the light from the window. "Merry Christmas," he whispered in her ear.

Christine felt her body stiffen, but she did manage a whispered "Merry Christmas" in response.

Laray then opened the door quietly and let them in.

Elizabeth's head lifted immediately.

"You finally finished? I should have stayed and helped."

"Nonsense. Sorry to keep you up so long. How's Danny?"

"Well," said Wynn, laying aside the newspaper, "it took half a dozen stories about the frozen North and the Indians, and a promise or two of a fishing trip—and a dozen of your mother's little lullabies. But he finally dropped off."

"I'm sorry," Christine said again. "You must be awfully weary."

"No need to feel sorry. We've had a lovely evening." Elizabeth stood, a contented smile on her face. "I've made some fresh coffee and cut some Christmas cake. Thought you might like it here by the fire."

Christine felt her face flush. She was trapped. There was no way she could send Laray away now without seeming very rude. She nodded, unable to say even a thank-you.

When she gathered her wits, she spoke quickly. "You'll stay and have some with us?"

"Your mother and I already celebrated the coming Christmas together," said her father, reaching for Elizabeth's coat. "Now it'll be good to get some rest."

"But it's Christmas," Christine pointed out, motioning toward the mantel clock.

Wynn laughed. "So it is. Well, Merry Christmas to you both." Then he leaned over and kissed Elizabeth on the nose. "And Merry Christmas to you, my dear."

Dad, don't start anything, Christine wanted to exclaim. But Laray made no move to follow suit.

"I'll get the coffee," he said instead, and bidding the Delaneys good night, he headed for the kitchen.

Still feeling on edge, Christine removed her coat and wandered over to stare down at the fire. She did hope she would not have a difficult time getting him to leave. She was tired and in no frame of mind for any kind of intimate conversations or cozy chats. How was she going to handle this?

Laray was soon back with two cups of coffee. He placed one on the small table near Christine.

"I know you're tired," he said, putting his own cup down, "so I'll be on my way just as soon as I have a piece of your mother's Christmas cake."

Christine felt her shoulders relax, and she sat down as Laray returned to the kitchen for their cake.

"What did you like best about the day?" Laray asked as he handed Christine her plate.

She smiled. "Danny—I guess. Wasn't he cute?"

"Yeah. Danny really did take the tension from the whole affair."

"You find weddings . . . tense?" Christine looked at him over the rim of her cup.

Laray did not hesitate. "Yeah. Don't you?"

Christine shook her head. "I find them . . . beautiful."

Laray squirmed. "Yeah," he agreed, "when they're all over." He took a bite of cake and murmured appreciatively.

Christine stretched out tired feet to the fire. "Well, this one is all over. I can't believe I finally have the sister I've always wanted. And a cute nephew to boot. I just wish they didn't live so far away." Her voice turned wistful.

"So why don't you stay?" asked Laray.

"Sure—and just as soon as I managed to get settled, they'd up and transfer Henry." Christine smiled ruefully.

Laray nodded. That was most likely.

"You've lived with the Force for a long time," he observed.

"Most of my life."

"Do you ever—resent it?"

Christine was surprised by the question. "Never," she said emphatically.

He shifted in his seat. "Some women do."

It was a simple statement. One that Christine could not deny.

"And you liked the North?"

"I loved the North."

"Would you go back?"

"In a minute."

There was silence except for the crackling and spitting of the fire.

"I've thought I'd like to try the North," said Laray.

Christine took a quick breath, about to launch into an excited litany of the beauties and advantages of the North. But she closed her mouth firmly. Where was this conversation heading? "I think you'd like it," was all she said.

"Yeah, well—right now I like this here Christmas cake. But I think I've had enough, so I'd best get me off home to bed. I work the late shift tomorrow, so I'll need to be able to keep my eyes open. Hope it's quiet, being Christmas—but one never knows."

Christine was relieved as Laray set aside his cup and stood to his feet.

"Suppose I'll see you at the Christmas service?"

"Oh, I forgot," Christine groaned. "What time does it begin?"

"Eight-thirty."

"Eight-thirty—it means not much sleep. Why so early?"

"Because it's Christmas. Because kids get up at five, and dinner is at one." Laray chuckled.

"I'll be there," Christine agreed, "but I'm not sure my eyes will be open."

"I'll drop around and pick you up."

"No. No, the walk will do me good. Might even make me alert enough to know what's going on."

Laray chuckled again.

"But we were going to load those boxes," Christine remembered.

Laray was shrugging into his coat. "Don't worry about the boxes. I'll look after them."

He waved a hand her way and was gone.

Christine stared after him, then turned once again to the fireplace. Only embers remained, blinking and snapping among the ashes and charred bits of remaining log.

She needn't have been so worried. Laray had said or done nothing amiss. No hints at future alliance. No attempts at further compliments. No subtle drawing close to her. Nothing.

For a brief moment she wasn't sure if she was relieved— or disappointed.

———

It was some stirring about that awakened Christine. Momentarily she groped for its meaning as she struggled to consciousness. Henry was picking up Danny. She could tell by muffled sounds and voices that he was warning Danny to be quiet and not to awaken Auntie Christine. With a sleepy smile, she crawled from the bed and reached for her robe.

"So you made it?" she said with a yawn as she greeted the two in the hallway.

Danny's excitement could not be contained. "I'm going to the cabin to have Christmas with my mom and dad."

"I heard."

"Our very first Christmas," Danny exclaimed. "I've even got a present for Mommy. Daddy helped me shop."

Danny held up the gift he had purchased. Christine could tell he had wrapped it himself. Amber would be thrilled.

"What is it?" she whispered, in keeping with the moment.

"Can't tell. It's a secret," he whispered back in Danny fashion.

"But your mommy's not here."

He looked doubtful. Secrets were secrets. "Can't tell anyway."

Christine nodded and gave him a hug.

"You have a good time," she said. Danny intended to do just that.

"We'll be back for dinner," Danny promised. "Then Mommy and Daddy are going to go away on the—the *what* moon, Daddy?"

"The honeymoon," Henry laughed.

With a flurry of waves and good-byes, they left and Christine turned to the kitchen. Henry had already started a pot of coffee on the stove. She would get dressed. The coffee would be ready by the time she was back.

Christine had no trouble waking up. The walk to the church had her fully alert. True to his word, Laray already had removed the boxes for storage later. She could totally relax and give herself to the celebration service. She slid in beside her mother just as the organ began the first carol. In her heart was the feeling this was a Christmas to be long remembered.

CHAPTER EIGHT

Christine made one more trip to Danny's room to check on him before retiring. It had been another busy day, and she was weary. The next day was Sunday, and after the morning service, she would enjoy a day of relaxation and rest. Her folks, with Uncle Jon and Aunt Mary, were to leave in the afternoon for the drive back to Calgary. In a way Christine was reluctant to see them go. She wished she were going with them, at the same time she was looking forward to the week with her new nephew. But with no school classes for Danny to attend over the Christmas holidays, she just wasn't sure how they would fill their days together.

Danny was sound asleep, his new Christmas car tucked up close. Christine gently removed it and put it on his dresser. *Seems to me Henry would have been wiser to get you a teddy bear,* she thought to herself. *A much better bed partner.*

She tucked the covers over the chubby shoulders and left the room. She had planned to begin the new novel her mother had given her for Christmas, but she felt too sleepy to even think about it. With one last trip to the front door to make sure it was locked securely, she flipped off the light.

A car engine purred to life, and just as she peered through the curtain, a police cruiser moved off down the street. Had Laray been intending to call but changed his mind when the light went out? She stood in the darkened room and wondered once again if she was relieved or disappointed.

———

The days with Danny went better than Christine would have dared to hope. He was an easy child to care for. She did get a little weary of reading the same book over and over. And it was a bit tiring playing Snakes and Ladders a dozen times a day—but for the most part the two got on famously.

Either in the morning after a hearty breakfast or in the afternoon while the sun was at its best, they went out for a walk. Christine found herself making snow angels and drawing patterns in the whiteness. They tried to build a snowman, but the snow was too crisp and cold and wouldn't mold properly. They had to content themselves instead with heaping up piles for a make-do snow fort.

On Wednesday Laray appeared at the door. "How's it going?" he asked casually, and Christine nodded that things were just fine and invited him in.

"Good. I wondered if you were tired of your own cookin' yet."

"She's a good cook," piped up Danny, who was on the floor playing with his car.

Laray did not mention the cooking again but dropped on the floor beside Danny. "Hey—that's a swell car."

"My dad gave it to me. For Christmas."

"It's almost as good as my cruiser."

"Better."

"Well, maybe it is at that. Let's see."

Laray gave the toy car a careful inspection.

"I think you're right. It is better." He handed the car back to Danny. "Wish I had one like it. We could play cars together."

"You could use my old one."

"Now, there's an idea."

Danny ran to get his old car, and Laray flipped over and stretched out on the floor. Christine thought he looked tired. With Henry away, he had drawn extra duty. She took a chair nearby.

"How have things been going at the office? Any major—what do you call them—happenings?"

"Nothing too serious." He turned his head to look at her. "All the same, I'll be glad when the boss is back."

Christine spoke on sudden impulse and just as quickly regretted her words. "Look—why don't you stay and have supper with us?"

Now, why did I go and do that? she inwardly chided herself as she rose from her chair. Not that she was concerned there would be enough for three. She had made plenty. It was just that it might send Laray the wrong message.

But it was too late. He was already smiling. "You twisted my arm. I'd love to."

Danny came running back with his old car, which he handed to Laray. "My new one's lots more better," he said, sounding apologetic. "We can take turns."

"Hey, this one suits me just fine. I don't have to worry none about denting a fender."

Christine left for the kitchen. As she worked she heard the two playing. She wasn't sure which one was having more fun. A game of cars must be one thing that a fellow never outgrew.

The game continued right to the supper table. The cars

were parked only when they bowed their heads for grace.

Danny felt perfectly at ease with Laray, so he kept up a constant chatter during the meal. Christine felt relieved. At least she wouldn't have to try to make conversation.

Laray insisted on drying the dishes.

"It's fine," Christine protested. "You have to get back to work."

"I'm done for the day."

"Oh." There seemed little else to say.

But it wasn't as bad as she had feared. Laray talked easily about Henry and his work at the RCMP office. Christine found herself listening carefully to all the compliments paid to her older brother.

"He's always been like that," she found herself saying. "Conscientious and caring."

Laray hung up the dish towel. "I'd add another 'c' word. Confident. Not . . . not arrogant. But confident. It makes a big difference when your boss is sure of himself. I've never seen him in a flap yet. Delaney—Henry just calmly goes about doing whatever it is that needs to be done."

Christine wrung out the dishcloth, thinking about what Laray had said. She knew that traditionally the Mounties called each other by their last names. She briefly wondered if "Laray" was his first or last name. Then she said, "I've never really thought about Henry that way—but you're right. Maybe he learned that from Dad. That's the way Dad has always been."

"You have great folks."

Christine nodded. "They are."

"I lost my dad when I was six." It was said without emotion, yet the statement tore at Christine's heart. An image of little Danny flashed through her mind. What he had lost—and now had found.

"What happened?"

"He was a logger. Got caught in a jam."

"I'm so sorry."

"Mom married again—when I was seven."

Christine waited. Was the new father good—or bad—news?

"He was a good guy. Even saw that we got to church."

Relieved, she moved to place the dried dishes back in the cupboard.

"We got along okay—but it wasn't the same as having my dad. He fed us and clothed us and never mistreated us—but he didn't give us much attention. Guess that would have been too much to expect. Eventually there were five more kids added to the family. That's about as thin as love can spread."

Christine wished to argue, but she didn't know what to say or how to say it.

"Anyway, we made out okay. I've got two older sisters and an older brother and another two sisters younger than me. That was in the *first* family. We all turned out all right."

"That's a big family," commented Christine, mentally doing the arithmetic. "Eleven children. Wow!"

"It was a houseful."

Danny returned with a picture book. "Did you see this big truck? It hauls logs and stuff." He thrust the book toward Laray.

"Let's take a look."

They left the kitchen together, and Christine finished putting away the dishes and slowly removed her apron. She wondered what they were going to do with the rest of the evening. Surely Laray was not expecting to be entertained. She could hear him now adding another log to the fire. With a deep breath she steeled herself and walked in to join them.

She was surprised when he asked, "Anything you want to do? I'd be glad to look after Danny if you want to step out for some fresh air—or anything."

Christine thought quickly. She would welcome this unexpected "time off"—but she had no idea how she might
use the opportunity. The stores were by now all closed for
the day. There was really no one she knew here whom she
wished to visit. It seemed foolish to just go for a walk in
the dark. She finally shook her head.

"Then maybe we should all go for a ride. The roads are
good. We could drive to the outlook point and show Danny
the stars. I used to be a real nut about the night sky when
I was growing up. I spent hours looking for the different
constellations. No northern lights here, but we can see
some stars—like you could reach up and touch them."

Christine started to decline, but Danny was already
cheering. What good excuse did she have for disappointing
him?

She nodded, and Danny ran for his coat and boots.

It turned out to be a pleasant enough evening. Once
they left the lights of the town, the stars seemed to pop out
of the blackness. The farther they traveled, the brighter the
stars became.

"Wow," said Danny, leaning back to gaze upward out
his window. "They are really big. And so many. Did you
know there were so many?"

Laray smiled.

"Do you think there are hundreds?" Danny continued.

"Way more than hundreds."

"Did you count them?"

"No one has counted them."

"Bet God has."

"I think you're right."

"Do they got names?"

"Yeah, I think many of them do. Some were named even
before Job's time. He talks about them in the Bible, chapter
nine. Orion. The Bear. Pleiades. I'll show you."

Christine was impressed with Laray's knowledge of the Scriptures.

Laray pulled over and stopped the car. From their vantage point, the whole canopy above was on display. Not a cloud hid from view any of the myriad of stars that twinkled above them.

"Now, if we just had us some northern lights it would be about perfect," Laray commented.

"Perfect," repeated Christine.

"What are north'ren lights?"

"Northern," Christine explained. "In the North. Lights. Special lights that God has placed in the skies. They are all colors and they dance and . . . they aren't like the stars that just twinkle. They are . . . are whole . . . whole sheets of light that change and move and . . ." Christine stopped. How did one explain the northern lights to a small boy?

"Like lightning?"

"Something like lightning . . . but different. I guess there is really nothing like them to compare them to."

"I'd like to see them."

"Maybe one day your daddy—or your grandpa can take you there."

"I'd like that."

Christine was quick to caution, "That's not a promise. That was just a . . . a maybe . . . someday."

Danny nodded solemnly. Christine hoped he understood.

The astronomy lesson began in earnest with Laray pointing out and naming the various visible stars and planets. Christine was amazed at how much he knew. To help Danny locate what he was pointing to, he drew diagrams in the snow. "And this is Orion. The star points are like this and the outline of the hunter is here—like this."

Danny looked from the diagram to the skies. "I can see it," he shouted. "I see him. Right there. See."

"Look," Christine cried as a star went streaking down through the sky, leaving a long, bright tail in its wake. "A falling star."

Danny stood openmouthed until the last glimmer of light died away.

"Why did it do that?" He turned to Laray.

"I don't think anyone knows for sure."

"Where did it go?"

"It burns out—as it falls."

"Now God doesn't have that one anymore." Danny sounded so sad that Christine found herself reaching an arm around his shoulder. Even Laray seemed affected by the young boy's disappointment. It would not do to tell Danny that God had millions of stars. That one really didn't matter. Instead, Laray wisely turned the small boy's attention back to the ones still there.

Laray finally checked his watch. "Guess it's your bedtime." Christine couldn't believe how quickly the time had slipped by.

Danny knew better than to object. "Can we do this again?" he asked instead.

"Sure. Why not? The stars are up there every night."

"Sometimes we can't see them."

Laray took Danny's hand. "Sometimes we can't—but they're there all the same."

It was a quiet trip back to town. Laray did not suggest that he come in with them. He walked the two up to the door and waited until Christine had turned on the light, then bid them a good-night.

Danny was washed and pajama-clad and tucked in bed. Christine smiled at his evening prayer. Besides his usual entreaties, he had added one more. "And, God, please don't let too many of your stars fall, 'cause I like to look at them."

Christine kissed his cheek and tucked the covers around his chin.

Back in the living room she stirred up the fire and fed it another log. Not for the warmth needed, but for the comfort. For some reason she could not explain, she felt strangely lonely. She wondered if it had something to do with that falling star that had just been lost forever.

———————

Laray called the next day. "Since you were so kind and invited me to supper last night, I thought I should take you and Danny out tonight. How about it?"

It sounded appealing, but even as the words of acceptance were on her lips she wondered if she was being wise.

"From now on I have the evening shift until your brother is back again. This would be my only chance."

That settled it. She could not turn him down.

"That would be very nice," she heard herself saying.

"Good. I'll pick you up about six. Sound okay?"

"That will be fine."

Whether it was the fact that Christine did not have to busy her mind or her hands with supper preparations—or some other reason—it turned out to be a very long day.

She fussed over what to wear. She didn't want Laray to assume she thought this was an actual *date*. Nor did she wish to look so everyday that he might feel dinner out was unappreciated. At length she chose a black skirt and blue sweater. She left her hair down but clipped it back from her face. She knew it was Henry's favorite way for her to wear it.

She dressed Danny in a newer outfit, answering his many questions about why they were eating out instead of in the kitchen, laid their coats by the door, and prepared to wait.

A few minutes before six, the telephone rang. Henry was just checking. How was everything going? Good. And

Amber wished to speak with Danny.

Christine handed the receiver to an excited Danny, who immediately launched into a full account of all of the good times he'd been having with Constable Laray. Christine felt her face getting warmer by the minute. It sounded dreadful.

"And we are going out to the . . . the café place. In his patrol car. Tonight. He said."

Christine did not know if she should ask for the phone again so she might explain, or simply to retreat in humiliation.

When Danny did hand the receiver to her, it was Henry back on the line.

"Sounds like you're being well taken care of."

Christine felt her face flush even more. "Laray stopped by last night to see how we are doing. Supper was almost ready, so we invited him to join us. He and Danny played cars while I got the food on the table. Then we took a drive to show Danny the stars."

"Good," said Henry, but Christine could not stop herself from hurriedly adding, "He offered to take us out tonight—as a payback."

"He has to pay back?"

"No, of course not. But he . . . he thinks he does."

Christine heard steps coming up the walk. She didn't know whether to mention the fact to Henry or hope he'd quickly hang up. Danny settled it for her.

"He's here!" he called loudly. "Constable Laray is here."

"He's there now?" asked Henry.

Christine put a hand to her hot cheek. "He . . . he's just arriving." Danny was already opening the door.

"Good. I'll speak with him," Henry said. "Save me another call."

By the time the two men had finished talking police business, Christine had managed to get herself in hand. The flush had left her cheeks, and her hands had stopped their trembling. Still, she wished with all her heart that she had not accepted this invitation.

At the small restaurant, she was careful to put Danny next to her on her side of the table. She soon lamented her decision. That put Laray directly across from her. She felt his eyes on her even when she was not looking directly at him.

They ordered the pork chops with mushroom sauce, deciding it had the best chance of not being too spicy.

Danny thoroughly enjoyed the experience. It was obvious he was not used to eating out. When Laray gave him his own choice of dessert, he was almost beside himself. He finally settled for the strawberry ice cream on lemon pie. It sounded like a strange combination to Christine, and she shook her head as she watched the small boy dig in.

"Well, maybe he's discovered something," Laray said in answer, his voice low.

Back at the house, Laray once again did not suggest coming in, even though Danny coaxed him to come play cars. "The boss will be home in a few days," was his answer. "I have to be sure everything is shipshape."

"What's shipshape?"

"In good order. Like your aunt Christine keeps your house."

Danny was satisfied.

"When can you come play cars?"

"Well—that's hard to say. I have to work pretty steady now until your dad gets home."

"Aww." Danny's shoulders slumped in disappointment, and his eyes went to the floor.

"But, hey—we'll play cars again. You can count on it." Laray gave Danny a playful punch on the shoulder.

"I like him," Danny said as the door closed behind

them. Christine had no comment. The truth was, she had
not been able to sort out how she felt about Laray. She had
not felt so agitated or confused since those last unsettling
weeks with Boyd.

CHAPTER NINE

Henry and Amber arrived home to wild whoops and many hugs. Danny was ready to settle in with his new dad. Even so, he was not quite ready to give up his auntie Christine.

"Can Auntie Christine stay too?" he asked his father.

"That would be very nice," answered Henry, "but I think Auntie Christine has things to do."

Danny turned pleading eyes her way. "Do you?"

Christine pulled the small boy close. "Your dad and mommy are home now. You are all together. It's time for me to go back to the city and find a job."

"You can have a job here with me."

"That would be fun—but I need another kind of job. One I am trained to do."

Even as she spoke the words, Christine had nagging doubts. Would she be able to find something? Things had changed so since the war.

The war.

In all of the busy preparations for the wedding and the daily caring for Danny, she had given little thought to the war. Wouldn't it be wonderful if it were all over? If all the troops were on the way home?

But she didn't suppose that had happened. There would have been great celebration across the land if it had. She would most surely have heard of it.

The war.

Christine, ready or not, was soon to be returned to the real world.

The plan was for Henry to drive her to Calgary on Sunday afternoon. Laray called Saturday morning.

"This may... this could be out of line," he started, sounding nervous, "but I really would like a chance to see you before you go."

Oh my, thought Christine, *I didn't want this to happen.* Or did she? She wasn't quite sure.

"All right," she heard herself agreeing. "What did you have in mind?"

"I don't get off until ten tonight. Could we take a short drive afterward?"

"I ... I ... sure. That's fine."

"I know it's not what—"

"No ... it's fine. Really."

"Thanks."

The connection clicked off, and she stared at the phone in her hand.

––––––––

When Laray arrived a few minutes past ten, Christine was ready. They exchanged little more than nods as he led her to the car and helped her in. She felt butterflies flitting in her stomach and reminded herself that she was acting like a schoolgirl.

"So are you stopping off in Calgary or going right on home?" he asked as he put the car in gear.

"I still haven't decided. Aunt Mary has invited me to stay with them and look for work in Calgary. I really don't know what to do."

"Is there lots of work in Edmonton?"

"I don't know. I haven't tried—except for the one job I had."

"Henry said you didn't have much trouble getting that one."

"No . . . no, it worked out . . . quite well."

They drove east out of the town. Christine was relieved that Laray was not taking her to the lookout again. She could imagine that local couples frequented the place.

Laray shifted into high gear and looked her way. "If you don't mind, I'll just keep driving while I talk. I never was very good at—at saying my mind."

Christine nodded dumbly.

"Henry let me know that you've just . . . had a . . . a breakup. Gave a guy back his ring."

Oh no, groaned Christine silently. *What else did Henry tell you?*

She cast a quick glance Laray's way, but his eyes were on the road ahead.

"I'm sorry it didn't work out. Those things can be pretty tough."

Christine appreciated his understanding, but she didn't know what to say.

"Because of that I've . . . I've sort of backed off," he continued. "I went through that once myself. I know that it takes time. 'Course I found a way to let off steam, so to speak. I went out and joined the Force. It worked. I had plenty to think about."

Laray managed to give her a lopsided smile.

Again silence.

"Anyway—I won't push. I just want you to know that I think you're pretty special—though this might not be the right time to be saying it. I don't suppose I'll be seeing you again unless..."

He did not finish the thought. Christine could have finished it for him. She knew exactly what he was saying.

"So I thought," he said slowly, "maybe we should come to—well, to some kind of understanding. Have a little sign between us, you might say."

Christine turned to look at him. She swallowed and waited, wondering what he was going to suggest.

"I thought maybe if the time ever comes when... when you think you'd be ready to... to think about... you know... dating again and you think maybe... well, you know... then you can just drop me a note in the mail. Even if I'm transferred, I will make sure your brother always knows where to find me.

"You won't have to make any promises. I don't expect that. Just a little note saying things are going fine. I'll pick it up from there."

Christine wanted to weep. He was being so gallant. So gentlemanly. Part of her wished to tell him that she was ready now. But she knew that was not true. She was not ready for another relationship. It was possible she never would be. Her heart truly had been broken by the last venture of falling in love.

She became aware of tears coursing down her cheeks. She dug in her pocket for a hankie. She had to say something. She couldn't just leave this kind and thoughtful man with no response at all.

She wiped her face and blinked back further tears. "I'm sorry," she began, her voice trembling. "You are quite right. I am not ready... yet. I... I have no... no desire to get involved with someone again. Maybe someday. I don't know... but not now."

She blew her nose and began again. "I do want you to know that if... if I were ready... I think you are a very fine man, and I would be proud to have you ask me out. I mean that. Truly."

He smiled. "That's a high compliment. And all I can ask for . . . at the moment."

He reached for her hand, but he did not hold it for long. Simply gave it a little squeeze as if to seal their understanding and released it again. Then he found a spot to turn the car around and headed for home.

It was a quiet drive back. It seemed that everything had already been said.

"It is a pleasure to know you. I wish you only God's best—whatever that is." He spoke so sincerely that Christine feared she would weep again. She did manage to tell him that she wished him the same, and then he was opening the car door and coming around to help her out. There was no move to kiss her, no arm about her shoulder or claim on her in any way. When they reached the porch, he leaned to open the door, his face very close to hers. "Just drop a note," he whispered; then he was gone.

Christine was grateful no one was still up to observe her entrance. She was crying so hard she could scarcely see her way to the room she was to use for one last night. He was so sweet. Was she making the biggest mistake of her life to walk away? But she wasn't ready to give her heart. Surely—surely if this was meant to be, the future would work it all out.

But Christine's pillow was damp before she managed to fall asleep.

————

Danny rode along for the trip to Calgary. Amber had intended to join them, but the onset of a head cold kept her at home. "You'd best stay in and take care of it," Henry had advised.

Christine was glad for Danny's chatter. It meant Henry would be less likely to notice her silence. Thankfully he asked no questions concerning the previous night, and Christine volunteered no information.

When Danny stopped for a breather, Henry turned to Christine with the same question Laray asked. "Will you be staying on in Calgary—or going on home?"

"Well, I'll need to go on home regardless. I brought nothing with me but this one suitcase."

"You might look for work in Edmonton again?"

"I think I may at least start there."

"Might be for the best. You know the city."

"Actually, I know very little of the city. I just traveled from my rooming house to work or church—that's about the extent of it. And I don't care to find work again in the same area."

She knew he did not have to ask why.

"What would you prefer to do?"

"Prefer? I'd prefer to go back home. Up north."

"You still feel that way?" Henry sounded surprised.

"I do."

"But there's nobody there now."

"All our friends are still there."

"Things have changed by now, Chrissy. It wouldn't be the same."

"It's still the North. That will never change."

Christine thought again of the constant cry of the North. There would be no emotional struggles to sort out would-be suitors. No disturbing war news. How she longed for its sense of peace. Of sameness.

Danny's head fell over against her shoulder. He had fallen asleep. She turned to rearrange him and pull him closer.

"Poor little guy. He's tuckered out."

"We really appreciate your looking after him. He's

grown very fond of his auntie Christine."

"I've grown fond of him too. I just wish—"

"Yes?"

"That we were closer. Who knows when I'll see him again?"

"Work in Calgary. Then you can come down every now and then."

"Then you'll go and get transferred to who knows where."

Henry chuckled. Any Mountie recognized that constant possibility.

"Did you know Amber is putting the shop up for sale?"

"No. When?"

"Soon. We have no idea how long it might take to sell, but we do want it all settled before that next transfer comes—whenever it is."

"I guess that's wise," Christine agreed.

For several minutes they rode in silence. Christine found her thoughts going back to Laray. How would he feel if Henry got transferred out? Of course it could be Laray who was transferred first. Who knew? She wished she could talk to her big brother about Laray, but she had no idea what she would say. For that matter, she had no idea how she really felt. It was all one confusing big lump in her chest.

———

She said good-bye to Aunt Mary and Uncle Jon and left for home the next day. The train ride was not nearly as enjoyable with no one to share it. She noted Lacombe, thinking about the fact that, except to visit family, her mother had never returned to the town. But then, maybe there was nothing in Lacombe to draw one back—not like the North, where she had grown up.

She had to spend a night in Edmonton before catching her ride to Athabasca. There was nothing to do and nowhere to go, so time dragged. She was glad when it was a reasonable hour to go to bed. But even then she could not sleep.

Henry had asked what she would do if she had the choice, and she had answered honestly. She would go north again. Without a moment's hesitation she would go back to the area of her birth. She belonged there. Had never fit well in the city or even the small town. Yet it was unreasonable to think that she could go alone. What could she do to earn her way? There certainly was no need for secretaries or stenos in the North, at least not that she was aware of.

She thought again about Laray. He had said he'd like to try the North. He had also said that all she had to do was write a note. Just a note.

But Christine pushed the idea from her thoughts. That would not be fair. It would not be right. To take advantage of his interest in her just because he could fulfill her dream. She would never be able to live with herself were she to do such a thing.

But she would pray. God knew the desire of her heart. Perhaps God could work out a way to get her back to the part of the country that she loved.

It was into the morning hours before Christine finally managed to quiet her thoughts enough to sleep.

She had to be up early. Mr. Carson, the same truck driver whom she had ridden with before, would transport her back home. He hauled goods back and forth between Edmonton and Athabasca.

Big and burly and unshaven, Mr. Carson was friendly enough. "How was yer trip?" His voice was deep and gruff. Christine might have been a bit afraid of him had she not known that her father trusted him.

"It was fine," she answered.

"Thought you might stay out."

"No. No, I intended to come home when I left."

"Yeah—but lotsa folks change their minds once they git out to civilization."

"I didn't see anything too civilized," she responded. "There was lots of war talk."

"Yeah. We're gitting it too. Wisht someone would jest sit on thet there Hitler. Whittle him down to size."

Christine wished it too.

"Another one of the hometown boys has left. S'pect there won't be any left around by the time this here thing is over and done with."

"Who?" asked Christine.

"Clem Carlson."

"Clem? I thought his name was Eric."

"Clem's the younger one."

"Clem? I didn't think they were taking them that young."

"He's a big kid fer his age. I think he lied some."

Someone should have stopped him. Told the truth about his age. I'm sure he's barely seventeen. Much too young to be shipped off to war.

"Guess there's lot of 'em doin' it. Lyin' about their age so they can go."

Christine was shocked. It was bad enough that those of age were going.

So even at home she was not to escape the war. Perhaps there was no place on earth where one was not touched by it.

But Henry is not going. Henry is needed at home. That fact brought her some consolation.

"'Spectin' another storm later tonight, so's I aim to push it some," the driver told her. And push it he did. Christine was glad she had been warned.

At one point she was sure they were going in the ditch.

They were coming down an incline much too fast when the truck hit a patch of ice. Whirling, spinning, swaying from one side to the other, the big man fought the wheel, this way, then that, then back again. Snow flew, making it difficult to see. Tires squealed and the load shifted.

When the truck finally stopped with its nose still pointed in the right direction, Christine slowly let out her breath. The big man seemed totally unruffled. " 'Bout used up all the road on thet one," was his only comment.

Christine opened her eyes and gradually unclenched her fists. She looked down at her knuckles and watched as the color slowly seeped back into them. It was taking even longer to get the air back in her lungs.

They pulled into town just as the sun was setting, and true to the man's prediction, a wind had come up and it was beginning to snow. "Gonna be real nasty in no time," the driver said. "Made it jest in time."

Christine nodded, thankful to be home in one piece. Thankful they weren't back in the ditch, helplessly and hopelessly stuck in the storm.

As soon as the truck pulled up in front of the house, she saw her mother brush back the kitchen curtain and look out into the semidarkness. By the time Christine had retrieved her suitcase, the door was open and her mother was waiting for her.

"How were the roads?" were her first words before Christine was halfway up the path.

"They were quite passable."

"Oh, I'm so thankful you are here. They are forecasting another bad storm."

Christine gave her mother a one-armed hug to avoid putting her suitcase down in the snow. "So I was told," she said wryly.

"Well—you're here now, so no need to worry. Your father will be home any minute. He'll be relieved too."

As Christine moved through the door she was greeted by Teeko. His long tail whipped back and forth, nearly knocking the plant from the small hall table.

"Settle down, Teeko," she scolded gently as she set her suitcase down and took the dog's face in her hands. "Were you lonesome? Did you miss everyone when we were gone?"

"You should have seen him when he saw your father," laughed Elizabeth. "He very nearly turned himself inside out, he was so excited."

"He doesn't look like he has suffered any." Christine rubbed a hand along the dog's back.

"I'm sure the boys from the office took good care of him. But he does miss your father when he is gone."

Christine moved on to her bedroom, suitcase in hand.

"So how did you and young Danny manage?" Elizabeth called after her.

"Good. He's a sweetheart."

"And all went well for Henry and Amber?"

Christine was at her door. "I didn't hear any complaints," she called back over her shoulder.

She took her time unpacking and putting away her things. In the kitchen she could hear her mother stirring about, putting the finishing touches on the evening meal. Teeko came to her door once and whined for some attention. When she did not respond he left again, probably to sit by the door and wait for Wynn.

Christine knew the moment her father was walking up the path. Even from her bedroom, she heard Teeko's excited yip and the thrumming of the massive tail. Wynn would soon be in.

"Heard from Christine?" were his first words.

"She's here."

"Already. I thought they'd be another hour at least. It's getting pretty bad out there. The wind has shifted and is blowing strong. It'll be a nightmare out in the open."

"Well, thank God, she's already here. Safe and sound."

Christine heard water being poured. Her father was washing for supper.

Just as she turned to leave her room and go join her parents, she heard it. The wind was reaching a fever pitch, already moaning and crying as it swept around the house and pulled at the troughs under the eaves. Something flapped, then quieted. Then flapped again. She hoped it was of little consequence, whatever it was, and would not be ripped away in the storm.

She entered the kitchen just in time to hear her mother say, "This is the first bad weather we've had since before Christmas. That must be some kind of record."

Wynn straightened, wiping his hands on the thick cotton towel. "Has been an unusually good winter so far. Not often we get so many storm-free days in a row."

He turned to look at Christine. "Hi, Peanut. Glad you're home." He smiled and hung up the towel. "How did your time with the new nephew go?" He crossed the room to give her a hug.

CHAPTER TEN

It was time for Christine to get serious about looking for work once again. Her mother was reluctant about it at first, but she finally accepted the fact. Christine decided to try Edmonton. This time she would be totally on her own. She was beginning to look forward to the challenge, but at the same time she felt just a bit nervous. What if she couldn't find a job? What if there were no proper rooms to rent? She calculated that she had enough funds to pay for a week in a hotel before she would need less-expensive housing. Would a week be enough to get settled?

Wynn arranged for her ride into Edmonton with their friend the truck driver. Christine wondered if her father would do so with such confidence if he had ridden with them on the last trip home. Well, there was really little choice. If one wished to get to the city, Big Sam Carson and his cartage truck was about the only possible way.

Christine packed up her clothes and the few belongings she wished to have with her and tidied her small room for the last time.

Teeko seemed to sense something unusual was taking

place. He paced the hallway, his eyes alert, his normally waving tail still and carried low. Occasionally a whine, more like a moan, escaped his throat. He looked as if he was already grieving the loss of a family member.

Wynn arrived home shortly before ten o'clock, the scheduled time for Christine to be picked up. He eyed the stacked boxes and suitcase set out by the door and asked, "You're sure you have enough money?"

Christine nodded. She wasn't really sure, but she did want to manage on her own now.

"If you need anything—"

"I know. Call home." Christine smiled.

Wynn nodded.

They had prayer together, seated in a circle, fingers interlaced. Christine knew this would not be the last prayer her parents would utter on her behalf. It was a comforting thought.

Wynn had just pronounced "Amen" when they heard the roar of the truck.

"The roads should be fine," her father told her, probably as much for Elizabeth's sake as her own. "Sam said they have cleared them out since the last storm. The weather's supposed to be good for the next few days at least."

Elizabeth began her recital of "don't forgets" and "be sure to's," as Christine listened and nodded. She had heard them all before, but she loved her mother for her concern.

"Phone as soon as you have news" was Elizabeth's concluding instruction.

The men loaded the things in quick order, and then there was the final round of hugs and promises. Christine climbed up into the truck with the help of her father's hand, waved one last time, and they were off.

Her last glimpse of her home was of her uniformed father standing with one arm about the waist of her mother, the other lifted in a final wave. Elizabeth did not lift a hand.

Hers were both busy wiping her eyes with a white hankie. Teeko stood beside them, tail drooping, head held high as though he was straining forward. Christine could imagine the mournful whine coming from his throat. It was all she could do to keep her composure. Had not Big Sam spoken she might have succumbed to tears.

"Better roads this time and no storm in the works. All the same, I hope to make good time."

Christine braced herself for another unnerving ride.

———

The first thing Christine did in Edmonton was get a hotel room. The King Edward would have depleted her limited resources in only a few nights, so she found a small hotel in the downtown area. It seemed central to the businesses and would make most places within walking distance. Once she settled in her room, she went to the lobby, purchased a paper, and spread it out before her on the table where she was having a bit of supper.

There wasn't much in the help-wanted ads that looked promising. She circled two and told herself she would make contact first thing the next morning.

In the meantime, she decided to make inquiries from anyone who might be available. The first prospect was the waiter. As he set her soup before her, she mustered up her courage and asked timidly, "I'm looking for work. Do you happen to know of anything—?"

"They did have a sign up for the afternoon shift—for a dishwasher." He didn't even look at her as he answered. Just set her soup down—a bit sloppily—and turned to go. Christine studied the soup stain on the tablecloth and shook her head. Dishwashing was not really what she had in mind, but it might well be what she would need to do.

She ate her soup—what was still left in the bowl—along

with a slice or two of less-than-fresh bread, drank her tea, and counted out the cash for the meal. She had to be careful until she was sure of employment.

At the lobby desk she stopped long enough to inquire of the bald gentleman with the round-rimmed spectacles, "Would you happen to have heard of any position openings? I'm looking for work."

He did not grace her with an answer. Just shook his head and went back to the newspaper he was reading.

She shrugged her shoulders and went on up to her room. If she was to find work, she was on her own. There didn't appear to be much help coming from elsewhere.

Christine was not sure if it was the evening soup or her own butterflies that made her stomach feel queasy, but she had a hard time getting to sleep. She was half tempted to dress and go down to the lobby and make a call home. Just hearing the voices of her mother and father would have a calming effect. But the thought of the long-distance charges kept her in bed.

For some strange reason she thought of Laray. *Just drop a note.* It seemed such an easy thing to do. He would even be willing to go north, he'd said. And he was a nice young man. And, more importantly, he shared her faith. So why was she hesitant?

She knew the answer. She was only interested in him because of what he might be able to give her. She would be using him. That wasn't the right premise for beginning a relationship that one hoped would lead to a solid marriage. She couldn't do it. She just couldn't. If she were to marry a man just to get her own way, she would always have feelings of guilt. What kind of relationship could be built on that? She had come so close to making one dreadful mistake. She wouldn't allow herself to make another.

He deserves much better than that, she lectured herself. She could never do that to him.

Then her thoughts turned to Henry, the big brother she had always loved and admired. Henry had been patient and allowed God to lead. And look now. Henry was so happy with his Amber and with his new son, Danny. Sure, there would undoubtedly be trials ahead, but they were committed to working them out together. That was what marriage was meant to be. An equal partnership. An attitude of love and respect, of coming together to give, not to get.

Christine tossed and turned, struggling with many thoughts and doubts. At last she climbed out of bed and knelt on the faded carpet. The room was chilly, but she paid it little mind. There was only one place to go with all of her turmoil. Only One who could bring any right direction to her in her confusion. Christine began, "Father, I need your help...."

———————

It was even colder in the room when she arose the next morning. She hadn't slept long enough, but once she had gotten there she had slept well. For that she was thankful.

She had her heart set on a good hot bath to help take the chill from her limbs and get her day started, but a trip to the bathroom down the hall left her disappointed.

The tub was chipped and stained and totally uninviting. She knew she must use it, but she would not be lingering there. No long soaks like her mother had enjoyed on their recent trip together.

Christine leaned over to turn on the tap. The water drizzled out. No matter how long she ran it, the temperature did not increase. She would be having a tepid bath, if indeed she could get the water even that warm.

She bathed hurriedly with no incentive to linger. She quickly dressed in what she hoped would be a fitting outfit for a job interview and took the stairs to the hotel's street-level floor.

She ordered toast and coffee. The toast was cold and stale and the coffee bitter—not at all like her mother's. She ate breakfast in the same manner she had taken her bath. It was a necessary chore before starting her day. Clasping her purchased newspaper close, she took to the street.

The morning chill was sharp. She pulled her collar up about her face and tried to twist away from the wind as she walked. She almost bumped into a hurrying gentleman in a dark overcoat. He mumbled something Christine did not wish to hear and hurried on.

The first place of business was farther away than she had expected. By the time she arrived, she was chilled to the bone and wished she had spent the money on a streetcar.

The place looked promising enough. She found herself hoping she would be successful.

The small office included just one desk. A woman sat behind it studying long, polished nails.

"Excuse me," Christine said after a few moments.

The woman turned her gaze to survey Christine from head to toe. She tipped her head but did not speak around the chewing gum in her mouth.

"I came about the ad in the paper."

The woman looked blank.

"The position. For a secretary."

"Oh, that." She waved a hand with a flash of her nails. "It's taken."

"Taken?"

"Yep. That's what I said."

"But it was in last night's paper."

"Look—it's taken. All right? I got it."

"You. . . ?"

The woman nodded nonchalantly while working the gum even more diligently.

"I see," said Christine as she backed slowly toward the door. But she didn't see. Not really.

Christine went back to the street and managed to spread out her paper against the wind. She located the next address and started to trudge through the whipping snow once again.

She didn't see a streetcar, and this turned out to be a walk of several blocks also. Her face felt numb by the time she arrived. She wondered if her cheeks were red or frost-bitten white.

The building did not look as pleasant as the previous one. In fact, things seemed rather tacky. The floor was dirty, the curtain at the window bedraggled and hanging in a lop-sided fashion, the chairs in the waiting area worn and askew. She wasn't sure she even wanted to have a job in such an office. But she needed the work. She took a deep breath and approached the desk where an elderly, tired-looking woman presided. She looked up from bespeckled, watery eyes and asked in a weary voice, "Yes?"

Christine felt an immediate sympathy.

"I'm here about the ad in the paper. The position for secretary."

The woman's eyes brightened. "Oh yes," she said, and was soon on her feet.

She crossed to a door and rapped. When there was a gruff call from inside, she opened the door and put in her head around it. "A woman here to see about the job." She sounded excited.

"Send her in." There didn't seem to be the same excitement there, however.

"Go right in," the woman invited, and Christine proceeded forward without even pausing to remove her coat.

An elderly man looked up from the papers on his desk. His expression was not inviting. "Just as I feared," he mumbled.

Christine had no idea what the man was fearing.

"You fresh out of school?" he grumbled.

"No, sir. I've had experience. I've—"

"So why you looking for work? You fired?"

What could she say? She was fired—in a way. She certainly wasn't going into a lengthy explanation of her broken engagement to the boss's son.

"There were . . . circumstances. . . ."

"Circumstances? That's what they all say. You didn't do your job. That's why folks get fired. Young people nowadays don't seem to realize that. You gotta learn how to do a job if you want to keep it."

"Yes, sir," Christine managed, her eyes lowering to the stain on his office floor.

"My wife's been doing this job for forty-three years. Never been fired. Forty-three years, mind you. Never had to look for another job her whole lifetime. That's the kind of worker I want here."

"Yes, sir," said Christine again, feeling like a child being scolded for breaking rules on the school playground.

He waved a hand at her, then toward the door. "I'm not looking for some young thing to pretty up my office. I want someone who knows how to work."

Christine took that as her dismissal. She nodded his direction and turned to the door.

As she passed the desk with the slump-shouldered woman, she noticed that her face looked downcast again. *You poor soul,* Christine thought. She was tempted to stop and offer the elderly woman a comforting hug, but she dared not. She might start them both weeping.

Christine had nothing to do but to face the wind again. All the long, long way back to her plain little hotel. Where were the streetcars when one needed them?

She decided to stop in a small café for a bite of lunch. Perhaps a cup of hot coffee would warm her up.

A sign in the window announced, "Experienced Waitress Wanted." She was tempted to offer her services. She could start immediately. But she wasn't experienced. She would very likely be turned down flat. She couldn't take another rejection. Not so quickly on the heels of her morning's disappointments.

Christine had no good news to share when she went to the lobby to call home, but she had to talk to her parents. She felt so alone. So isolated. And so deflated. She tried not to let her mood show as she reported on the weather and Edmonton and the room she had at the hotel, but she was quite sure she was fooling no one.

"Are there jobs, dear?" asked her mother eventually.

"Well, I've been buying the paper and checking things out. There are jobs available—but so far none of them have worked out. I'll keep trying. I'm sure the right one will turn up."

She hoped her voice managed to carry a hint of optimism.

"I'm sure it will. Those things take time."

They chatted of other things. Elizabeth had received a letter from Henry and Amber. Each had written—it was so sweet. And even young Danny had signed his name and added some hugs and kisses.

There were changes at Henry's office. Sergeant Rogers had been transferred out—to some place in B.C. A new recruit had been sent in, and Henry was busy teaching him the ropes. He wasn't sure yet how the new fellow would make it. He seemed to have a chip on his shoulder.

So Laray is still there, thought Christine. It was unlikely he would be transferred anyplace soon with one new recruit already in the office.

"Henry is so thankful to have the steadying influence of Maurice," were her mother's next words. Her mother had always refused the traditional use of officers' last names.

They are people, she had argued over the years, *not just police-men.* So if they were young, she called them by their first names. If they were older, she referred to the Mountie by his last name and rank.

"Yes," murmured Christine, "I'm sure he is."

"They think they have a buyer for the barbershop. Amber is quite excited about it. She says she will be only too glad to hang up her scissors. Henry says she's not getting off that easy. After becoming used to the job she does, he won't let anyone else touch his hair." Elizabeth chuckled.

Christine was thinking about the cost of the call. Just hearing her mother's voice was such a comfort, but she really could not afford to continue. "I'd better go, Mom. This is adding up," she finally said.

"Is there a way we can phone you?"

Christine found the number of the hotel and hoped the receptionist would handle a call. Then she bid her good-bye and hung up.

She wasn't sure if she felt better or worse as she climbed the stairs to her room. It had been good to talk, but now her loneliness seemed even more intense.

It will be different once I find a job, she promised herself. *Then I will meet new people and have some contacts.*

What she must do immediately was find a church home. That would give her a connection that she sorely needed. She was glad that Sunday was only two days away. Surely there was a church within walking distance. Somehow she would find it.

Christine did find a church, large and beautiful and filled with worshipers. She felt rather out of place when she stepped into the wide foyer on that first Sunday. But an elderly usher greeted her warmly as he presented her with the morning bulletin. She received many smiles and nods as she took her seat in the pew to which she was directed. The people seemed genuinely friendly. *Thank you, Lord,* she prayed as she bowed her head before the opening hymn.

The music did more than lift her spirits. It touched her very soul. She felt the heaviness of the past few days drain away from her and found herself totally ready for the morning's sermon.

The kindly-looking minister in his aristocratic robes spoke engagingly but also from the heart. Christine felt drawn to God as she listened to the familiar account of the ten lepers, told in a refreshingly new way. She would be back. She had found a church home.

But as she left the sanctuary, she longed for more than a nod, a smile, and a handshake. She longed for friendship. Conversation. Maybe even an invitation to dinner.

"Those things take time," she heard her mother's voice. Christine knew it was true. But in her loneliness she prayed it would not take too long.

CHAPTER ELEVEN

Throughout the next days, Christine trudged the city streets following one empty lead after the other. Her funds were getting dangerously low and her spirits even lower. She began to fear she would need to concede defeat and return home. The thought was both inviting and humiliating. It would be good to again be surrounded by family love and support, but it would be very difficult to admit that she was not able to make it on her own.

And then the daily paper had a promising ad. *Wanted. Reliable person for well-established city business office. Must have typing and shorthand. Some experience preferable, but willing to train.*

It sounded perfect. She could hardly sleep for excitement. That night her prayers were more specific. She really wanted—*needed*—that job.

The next morning she was up early and hurried through her frigid bath. She wanted to be the first in line at the office for the coveted position.

When she arrived at the office building, the doors were not as yet opened. She paced back and forth, stomping her feet and clapping her hands for warmth. At length a gentleman with a key appeared. He unlocked the door, gave Christine a brief glance, then entered without a word. The door clicked shut behind him with a sound of finality. But she refused to give in to her flip-flopping emotions.

It was not long until another well-dressed businessman appeared. He too had a key. He even gave Christine a nod and wished her a good morning. She moved a step closer to the door but was not invited to enter.

A woman arrived, so bundled in furs and scarves that Christine could not see her face. She pulled a key from her handbag and opened the door.

"Excuse me," Christine dared say. "I'm here concerning the ad in the paper. For secretarial help."

"We don't open until nine."

"Is there . . . is there someplace where I could wait . . . out of the cold?" Christine inquired bravely.

The woman hesitated, then nodded her head. "I suppose it would be all right."

She held the door and Christine entered, grateful for the warmth that rushed to meet her.

"You can use one of those chairs over there," she gestured. "I'll call you when Mr. Stearns is ready."

But as the morning wore on, Christine did not receive a call. It was almost noon before she got up courage to look for someone who might help. She walked down a short hall.

There was the woman, busily handling both a phone and several sheaves of paper. Christine waited patiently until the phone was cradled.

"Excuse me. I was to see Mr. Stearns."

The woman, startled, stared at Christine, her eyes wide. She ran a hand across her forehead in agitation. "Oh, gracious," she said, "I forgot all about you." Her tone indicated that Christine was indeed an intrusion into her busy day.

Christine refused to cower.

"I was to see Mr. Stearns," she repeated.

"He has just left for a luncheon engagement. You'll have to come back." There was no apology in the voice.

"I'll wait," said Christine firmly. And wait she did. This time she did not return to the seat in the outer lobby. She took a chair in full view of the receptionist. She did not wish to be forgotten again.

Almost two hours later Mr. Stearns returned. He was younger than either of the two men whom Christine had seen enter the building.

The receptionist watched him remove his hat and hang up his coat.

"There is an interviewee here to see you, sir," she said abruptly. The man cast a quick glance Christine's way, then spoke to the woman. "I'll let you know when I'm ready."

It wasn't what Christine had wanted to hear. Before she could stop herself she was on her feet. "Sir," she said, her voice sounding more forceful than she intended, "I have been here since before nine o'clock this morning, and if this job is not available, I'd appreciate the courtesy of your telling me so I can look elsewhere."

He looked at her a moment, a slight smile at the corners of his mouth. "Come on in," he said finally with a nod of his head. He led the way into his office.

Christine took the chair indicated. Her face still felt flushed from her recent upset. She sat stiffly, nervously fingering her handbag. She was sure any chance she might have had was now forfeited.

Mr. Stearns was very professional with the interview, and before long Christine felt the tension leave her. She would enjoy working for this man. He was courteous, concise, and clear, and seemingly well organized. Just the kind of boss she could appreciate. *Oh, I hope I can get this position* kept running through her mind.

Though Christine did not ask, the salary was mentioned, more than she had dared hope. More than she had made when working for Mr. Kingsley. She would be able to afford decent living accommodations. The idea set her heart to racing.

At the end of the session, he stood and reached across his desk to shake her hand.

"Thank you for coming in, Miss Delaney. I have two more appointments with other interviewees set for tomorrow morning. I must follow through with those, even if they are a mere formality. If you'll leave your phone number with the receptionist on the way out, I'll see that you are promptly called."

Appointments, mused Christine. *I should have thought to make an appointment.* Well, that was a lesson learned for next time—should there be a next time.

She thanked Mr. Stearns and stopped at the desk on her way out. The receptionist surprised her by giving her a smile—even though it looked rather weary. "I do apologize for taking so much of your time," she told Christine. "I'm just so . . . so overloaded here."

Christine returned the smile. "I'd like to be able to help ease your load," she said sincerely.

The smile brightened. "I'd like that too. I hope you get the job."

Christine left the number of the hotel and started out for the return to her room. Though the day was still cold, she felt a warmth inside that lifted her spirits considerably. She felt that her prayers were possibly being answered. She was even thankful that God had spared her from one of the other jobs she had explored. They were not anything in comparison to the possibilities of this one.

Of course, she knew nothing at all about the other candidates. Perhaps they were far more skilled and had much more experience. Still, the interview had gone well. She had been relieved that Mr. Stearns was so easy to talk to. So relaxed, yet efficient and professional. He had put her at ease almost instantly. *Mr. Stearns is not stern,* she quipped to herself as she walked. She hoped—oh, she so hoped—that the position would be hers.

She was awfully tempted to telephone home with her great news. But she held herself in check. She would not call until she could actually say that this ideal job was hers. At the same time she reminded herself that though it wasn't a given as yet, she felt confident. She would know soon. Tomorrow, after the other morning interviews. The receptionist had promised to call by ten o'clock.

For now all she could do was wait and pray.

Christine was just preparing for bed when she got a message that her mother was on the telephone. She hurried down to the lobby and the shared public phone.

"I'm sorry to bother you so late," her mother apologized. "I just had a call from your uncle Jonathan. Aunt Mary has had a nasty fall. I thought you'd want to know."

"What happened?" asked Christine, feeling her heart constrict.

"She slipped on some ice. The doctor says nothing seems to be broken, but she's going to need bed rest for at least a few weeks."

Christine went cold. "Bed rest? So she will be at home?"

"That's what Jonathan said. He's not sure how they'll manage. The girls can't come, what with little ones at home. Jonathan says he'll have to try to find some day help. He can't leave her alone. It's not that he can't afford some-one—it's just that nursing help is so hard to find right now, with the war and all.

"I'll go." The words were out of her mouth before Christine could even check herself.

"Oh, but, dear—"

"It's okay."

"You haven't found a job?"

"I . . . I think I might have. They're to call me tomorrow. But it . . . it went well. Mr. Stearns said I have the right qualifications, and the receptionist seemed pleased."

"Oh, my dear—"

"No—it's all right, Mom. Really. If Aunt Mary needs me, then I'll go."

"But it sounds like such a good opportunity. This job. I'd hate for you to lose it."

"It's okay."

"Would the job still be there for you in a couple of weeks?"

Christine bit her lip. "I don't think so. No. The poor assistant is nearly out of her mind trying to keep up."

"I'm sorry. I'd go myself, but I—"

"No, Mom. This is the easiest solution and least upsetting to everyone," Christine said firmly. "Do you want to call Uncle Jon or shall I?"

"If . . . if you're sure . . . I'll call him. Tonight. You're sure?" Elizabeth asked again. "I wouldn't like you to jeopardize your career, Christine, and neither would your uncle Jon."

"Tell him I'll be down on tomorrow's train."

Christine scarcely heard any more of the conversation. Her thoughts were whirling, and her head was beginning to ache. Was she passing up an opportunity of a lifetime? She didn't know. Perhaps she wouldn't even have gotten the job. Maybe one of the other interviewees would be chosen. *But Mr. Stearns said he must go through with the appointments as promised. A formality, he said. Doesn't that sound like . . . like he's already made up his mind?*

Well, it couldn't be helped. Aunt Mary needed her. Surely she could trust God with the future.

———————

True to her word, the receptionist's phone call came right at ten. As Christine ran down to the lobby, she wasn't sure what she was hoping to hear. If the woman said, "I'm sorry, but you didn't get the job," at least Christine would feel she had not sacrificed a dream job for the sake of her aunt Mary. That God had known all along and was preparing something else for her. On the other hand, it would be another blow to her already fragile confidence if the receptionist informed her that they had decided she wouldn't do after all.

But it was an enthusiastic voice that greeted her on the other end of the crackling line. "You got the job—no contest," the woman enthused.

Christine shut her eyes tightly and bit her lip.

"Miss Delaney. Are you there?"

Christine managed to say that she was.

"You got the job."

"I'm . . . I'm so sorry. Something has come up. I just got a call last night. My aunt . . . she had fallen and will be bedridden. I . . . I need to go to care for her."

The line went silent.

"Your aunt?" the voice finally said.

"Yes."

Another silence.

"Here in the city?"

"No. No, in Calgary."

"So you have to go out of town?"

"Yes. I'm afraid so."

"For how long?" All of the enthusiasm had left the voice.

"I'm ... I'm not sure. At least for two weeks ... maybe longer. It depends."

"We ... we can't possibly wait for two weeks."

"I know. I'm sorry. I'm terribly sorry I ... I really wanted that job. Really."

A long sigh traveled over the phone line. "I'm sorry too. Mr. Stearns was so pleased with your qualifications, and I ... I really thought we could work well together."

"Thank you. I thought so too."

"There's no one else ... to go?"

"No. No ... we've already exhausted the list of possibilities."

"Well," the woman sighed again, "I guess there is nothing more to say except good luck, then. Sorry it didn't work out."

"Please ... please tell Mr. Stearns that I'm dreadfully sorry. I ... I appreciated his ... his consideration of me. I'm sure I would have enjoyed working for him."

"I'll tell him."

"And thank you. I ... I do hope you find someone to ... to help you out. Very soon. I'm sorry."

Christine felt numb as she replaced the receiver. *Why? Why did it happen like this?* She had asked God for a job, and the perfect one had come along—one she had just been offered. So why had Aunt Mary's fall come at just the wrong time? She would never understand. Never.

But Christine could not let herself wallow in self-pity for long. She had a train to catch and very little time to get to the station. She called a cab. She couldn't possibly walk and carry all her things. She counted out the cash in her purse. She would have enough for the cab fare and her train ticket and very little more. Once she got to Uncle Jon's, of course, she would have accommodations and food.

Swallowing her great disappointment, she hauled her suitcases and boxes to the lobby and stood near the door so she could watch for her ride to the station.

———————

Christine rested her head against the high seat back as many other travelers had done throughout the years. The uneventful train ride was giving her time—too much time—to think. This was not the way it was to work out. This was not what she had planned. Was there really a purpose in all of this? Was she doing the right thing? Surely she would have few opportunities for a job like the one she had just turned down. Was she making a dreadful mistake?

But could she really do otherwise? Was there any other reasonable choice? Wouldn't she be dreadfully selfish to put her own desires before the needs of a family member—one who had unselfishly given of herself to Christine's mother—and to Christine—over the years?

Round and round in her muddled brain the arguments and frustrations clamored. At length she breathed a simple prayer, "Lord, if I've done the wrong thing, the unwise thing, please forgive me. If I've done the right thing, please give me peace. I trust you, Lord, in this and in all things."

A calmness gradually settled over her being. She decided she would have been even more conflicted if she had taken the job and left Uncle Jon to work things out on his own.

Her sense of personal struggle was gone. There was still the feeling of disappointment but no longer the agitation that things "hadn't worked out." The Lord was in charge of her life.

The voice of the conductor awakened her. "Calgary. Next stop, Calgary," he was calling as he walked up the aisle to the gentle swaying of the train.

Christine, surprised that she had slept, stirred and gathered her travel bags to her side. She would not worry about what the future held, but she found herself wondering just how the coming days would unfold. Well, that was in God's hands. It was actually rather exciting.

Uncle Jonathan stood on the platform, peering into the faces of those who disembarked. When he saw Christine, a smile replaced the worry lines. Without a word he reached out to embrace her.

"I can't tell you how relieved we were to hear you could come," he said against her hair. "But I'm so sorry to intrude."

"Nonsense," Christine responded with a smile. "I'm glad I was available."

"Mary can hardly wait to see you. She's still in a good deal of pain, I'm afraid, with her back injured, but she puts on a brave front."

"I'm so sorry, Uncle Jon," Christine said with another hug.

"Yes. Well, these things happen. Not always to our good pleasure—but Mary has already found a whole list of things to be thankful for."

"Thankful?"

"She's thankful nothing was broken. That she didn't suffer frostbite as she lay on the sidewalk. That a neighbor happened along almost immediately. That she received good medical attention. That she doesn't have to spend time in hospital. That she has a warm, comfortable home. The list goes on. But most of all, she is thankful you were willing to come to be with her. That is number one on her list, I believe."

He smiled again.

Christine managed a smile of her own. She was awfully glad she hadn't said no to this opportunity. Surely, surely, God had everything else carefully planned out.

They soon had stowed her luggage in the car and were pulling away from the station. Jonathan continued filling Christine in on the situation at home. "She's not to move on her own at all, so it means she needs to be turned every few hours. The difficulty is to get her to relax and not try to help with the moving. She feels so bad about having to put someone else out in such a way. Mary has never been used to being waited on. She has always been the one to do the waiting. This is most trying for her."

Christine nodded.

"Of course we still have Lucy, and there's the lady who helps with the cleaning and laundry. But I've been told that bedside care is something else. The doctor just shrugged and wished me good luck. Says the hospitals are dreadfully short of nursing staff."

He steered the car through an intersection, then continued. "So your responsibility will be to look after Mary. Nothing else. There's not much she can do from her prone position, but she enjoys being read to if you feel you'd like to take that on. I work from eight in the morning to six each day. I will take over when I'm home."

He accelerated up the hill that led to his Mount Royal home. "I hope all this is not asking too much."

"No—not at all. I'll be glad to look after her."

"In this kind of situation I have always felt that the best policy is to have everything clearly understood right up front," her uncle went on. Christine nodded in agreement.

"I haven't had time to draw up anything on paper, but if you'd like, I can."

Christine was surprised. "No. No, that's not necessary."

"You'll be paid each month, with half a month's salary given in advance."

"Salary? Oh, I'll not take a salary. I came to help. My room and board will—"

"A salary. I wouldn't think of doing it any other way. It's a salary—or we send you right back." He glanced her way, eyebrow quirked.

Christine nodded dumbly. She had not even considered working for pay.

"Should you need a further advance at any time, for any reason, please do not hesitate to ask," Uncle Jon added, then told her the amount of the salary.

Christine gasped. "Oh, that's too much. Surely—"

"I've inquired into what would be expected for such a position. I've been assured that is the cost for such an employee. I wouldn't ask my own niece to work for any less."

"But I came to help—"

"And you don't know how thankful we are," he said as he turned to look at her once again. "I was so concerned about Mary. She was quite beside herself with the complications of her fall. You being here is truly an answer to our prayers."

There seemed to be little else for Christine to say.

She tiptoed up the stairs to her aunt's room. It seemed so strange to see her energetic aunt Mary lying still and white in the big bed.

"Aunt Mary," Christine whispered, and the woman's eyelids fluttered open.

"Christine. You've come, dear." A smile lit her face, and she reached out her hand.

"I'm here. I'll be back to tend to you just as soon as I get instructions from Uncle Jon. He says you are soon due for your pain medication."

"A pill. Yes. I look forward to it, I'm afraid."

Christine could see the pain in her aunt's eyes.

"I'll get you some fresh water and be right back," she promised.

"Thank you, dear."

Christine was at the door when her aunt spoke again. "Christine—I'm so glad you came. I really wasn't looking forward to spending my next days with a stranger. It'll be so nice to have you here, my dear."

Christine nodded, smiled, and left with the water pitcher.

CHAPTER TWELVE

Christine would not have denied that the next weeks tested her resolve to trust God with her circumstances. Though Aunt Mary was undemanding and cooperative, the days dragged tediously. Turning her aunt to avoid bedsores was one of the biggest struggles. It was accomplished by skillfully maneuvering the sheet on which the patient lay, but it was not easy for Christine to do alone. At times it took more than one attempt before it was successfully completed, and often the procedure was accompanied by pain. Christine tried to time the event so the medication was most effective.

Jonathan installed a bedside bell that rang in Christine's room and in the main hall, so while Mary slept, Christine was free to stretch her legs and catch a few minutes of rest herself. But Mary slept very little the first days. The pain was simply too intense and the spasms in her back too severe. Christine alternated hot and cold compresses to help relieve the pain, but even they were not very effective.

Christine read until she was hoarse, mostly in the hopes that the rhythm of words would be a distraction. She wasn't sure if her aunt was really following the story.

Gradually, oh, so gradually, it seemed, the pain began to ease. Mary's face was not as pinched, her breathing not as shallow. She rested more easily between doses of painkiller. She did not need to stifle groans as much when she was turned. And though the doctor, who visited regularly, assured them that she was making good progress, he also warned that this was the most critical time. Once Mary was not in such intense pain, she was more likely to do something to aggravate the injury and slow down her progress. Christine became even more vigilant. She did not leave the room for little breaks or take her meals in the dining room or kitchen.

But her evenings were her own. At first she had no idea how to spend them, but then she became acquainted with two girls from the church who had gotten to know her situation. They soon invited her to become involved with them in helping out at the servicemen's center, working with young soldiers—men and women who were stationed in Calgary.

Christine was hesitant at first. What could she possibly do to be of help? But after one or two visits to the center, she discovered there were many things she could do—as simple as keeping a full pot of coffee available or setting out brownie squares. It was not long before she was fully involved many evenings each week, watching for ways to bring some kind of pleasure or relief to those in uniform.

Many were awfully young and not nearly as brave or confident as they pretended to be. Christine's heart ached for them, and she prayed with all her heart that she might be some encouragement, some measure of light to the ones who were walking into the throes of war without a personal faith.

It was not long before she discovered that many of the young men were notorious flirts. They seemed to hold the opinion that the only reason the young women volunteers were there was to meet some uniformed young Casanova for the beginning of a wild romance. Christine had no such intention, and she was continually having to make that plain.

In spite of the complications, Christine did love the work. Many of these young people had been swept into the military on a wave of public sentimentality or as an open invitation to adventure, to see the world. Few seemed to have given careful consideration to where their choice might take them, and they now were having second thoughts. Not that they would not have made the same choice at a more serious moment if they had felt their country was truly at risk. But the war seemed very far away. Britain might feel threatened by the march of Nazism—but Canada? It didn't seem too likely.

Every day the local headlines and radio stations broadcast news from the front. Many European countries were being invaded in Hitler's march to power. Britain and its Commonwealth countries seemed to be alone in trying to halt the destruction. This was serious business. This was not a holiday abroad. Young soldiers were giving their lives. Many were returning from battle with broken or mutilated bodies. Others had been taken as prisoners of war. Christine felt sure this really wasn't what these young enlistees had in mind.

She would not have attempted to downplay their sacrifice. Far from it. She admired them for the stand they had taken—providing that stand had been taken with an understanding of the potential consequences.

Night after night she listened to the stories of their lives, their secret fears—when they allowed themselves to be serious enough to talk openly. Silly pranks, machismo, and loud laughter often masked how they really felt. But when they did feel safe to share their deeper feelings, it was often an open invitation to point them to Someone who would go with them even behind enemy lines. Several of the young men and women turned up at Sunday services in the local churches.

But there were many more who did not. Who laughed in the face of impending danger and strengthened their own boldness with vulgar speech and swaggering stance. At times Christine wished to shake them into reality. But she knew that tack would never work. They needed love. They needed prayer. They needed a sense that there were those who would listen to them. The volunteers tried hard to supply as much support as they could.

The day finally arrived when the doctor allowed Mary out of bed for the first time. Christine could tell by her face that she still wasn't without pain, but she bit her lip and held back any comment. Weak from lack of muscle use, she needed support as she took her first steps to the chair that awaited her.

"As soon as we can we will start a regimen of exercise," the doctor said. "First we want to see how her back will respond to some time in the chair."

Within a few hours, Mary was ready to go back to her bed. But she had surpassed the doctor's first-day hopes. The next day she was up for a longer period of time, and the following day she spent almost half of her day in an upright position.

The doctor decided it was time to begin therapy to strengthen the muscles, and Christine was shown a series of movements that she was to help Mary accomplish several times a day. Christine occasionally wondered just who was getting the most exercise. Many nights she went to bed early, she was so weary. She even missed some evenings at the center. She was simply too exhausted to go.

But it was not long until Mary could assume most of the muscle stretches and lifts on her own. Barring complications, Christine knew she would not be needed much longer.

"Why don't you find a job here, dear?" Mary asked one morning as they worked together with the daily routine. "There must be lots of work available. Calgary is booming, they tell me. And many young people have enlisted and have been shipped overseas."

"I've been thinking about it," Christine admitted. "If I did find something here, I could stay involved with the service work."

Christine was feeling that what she was doing with the young recruits was beginning to have significant meaning. She believed she had found her niche in the war effort. By helping to prepare and fortify those who might end up in action, she was doing her part. Perhaps not in actual defense, but in speaking with the young men and women—those who would in the future be defending freedom—of the need for a personal faith in God. Eternal life was of even greater importance than temporary physical life. Christine believed that with all her heart.

There were plans in the making to start a second center. And talk of hiring a full-time chaplain to oversee the program. Ministers from various churches of the city had been donating what time they could afford. With a chaplain dedicated to the work, much more could be accomplished. The city churches would go together to pay the man's salary. It sounded like a wonderful idea to Christine.

"The work you are doing is so important," Aunt Mary was continuing. "I'm anxious to get back to my ladies' group to start filling CARE boxes again. I've missed being involved."

"Well, you have been able to take up your knitting,"

Christine reminded her. "I'm sure all those woolen socks will be appreciated by someone, somewhere."

"I'm going to talk with Jon. I think it's time for you to be released to look for that job. Maybe he will even have some suggestions."

Christine was excited. She was sure she'd never find a job quite as perfect as the one she'd lost in Edmonton, but no doubt God was at work in the whole matter. Had she stayed in Edmonton she would not have discovered the Hope Canteen program.

On the twenty-fifth of March, Christine approached the building that Jonathan had suggested for her first Calgary job interview. She was surprised that the whole venture still gave her nervous butterflies. This time she had made an appointment beforehand and came with Jonathan's reference in hand. She did hope that the interview would go as well as the one with Mr. Stearns and that she would find a boss as nice as he seemed to be.

The man behind the big desk seemed civil enough. Mr. Burns asked logical questions and outlined logical requirements. "I've known Jonathan for years, and I don't think he would recommend you if you couldn't handle the job," he said simply. "You can start Monday morning."

Christine could not believe it had come so easily—and so quickly. She thought back to those treks through the winter cold in Edmonton and her disheartened return at each day's end. Surely God was indeed in charge. She decided to stop on her way back to buy her aunt Mary a box of candy and her uncle Jon a new necktie. She had a job. She had money in her bank account. She had a place to live—if she still wanted to board with them. And, most importantly, she felt she was making a difference in lives. What more could she ask?

Why didn't she feel happy? Of course she was happy. No, she was content. She didn't feel really settled. She wondered if she would ever be truly happy until she was back in the North where she belonged. Anywhere else, she felt like she was just putting in time.

Her thoughts suddenly jumped to Laray. She had been much too busy to even think about him for many weeks. But now the days of caring for Aunt Mary were over. Now she could take up with her own life again.

What was Laray doing now? Had he been transferred? Henry had not said so. Nor had her mother mentioned it in any of their frequent phone conversations.

No, he must still be there. Was he still waiting for a note from her? Suddenly the thought of getting back in touch was appealing. She would like to know what was going on in his life. She wished he could pay a visit to the city. She would like to take him to Hope Canteen. Let him listen to the talk—some of it casual banter, some of it serious as one or another opened hearts about their hopes and fears. She would like Laray to be able to feel the pulse of the young people preparing to serve their country.

Just drop a note. Could she do that? But what would it signify? Would he be expecting too much? *"No promises,"* he had said. *"I'll take it from there."* What had he meant by that? And would he still feel the same way? It had been almost three months since they'd had the conversation. Things may have changed by now.

All weekend Christine thought off and on about writing the note. Once she even sat down with pen and paper. *"Just a note to say you are doing fine"*—wasn't that what he had said? That sounded easy enough. But she couldn't write it. She wished she could talk with Henry. Perhaps Laray might have said something—indicated in some way how he currently felt. But it wasn't the kind of discussion she could have with her big brother by phone. It just didn't seem right.

The note was never written.

———

Christine was pleased at how quickly she was able to get into her new office routine.

She decided she would accept Uncle Jon and Aunt Mary's kind invitation to be a boarder, at least for a while. They worked out their agreement as to rent, and Christine was sure she could never have made a better arrangement any other place. Nor would she have had more loving care—or better meals. She felt blessed.

All things work together for good, she often repeated to herself, though it was a wonder to her that God would allow her aunt Mary to endure so much suffering just to get her to Calgary. When she mentioned that fact to Mary, her aunt smiled.

"I don't think that's what the verse means—really," Aunt Mary replied thoughtfully. "I don't hold God accountable for my fall. It was my own carelessness. I knew the streets were icy, and I shouldn't have been hurrying so. But you know me. Jonathan is always telling me I need to slow down.

"But once it did happen—that was when God stepped in and made something good come of it. It could have been all just useless pain that accomplished nothing—but God saw to it that it brought about some good. I agree that you are here for a purpose. You have real gifts for helping and listening and sharing your faith that you are using at Hope Canteen. I think that is God's place for you at the present. What He has in mind for the future, I have no idea. But He'll let you know that in plenty of time to prepare for it."

Christine nodded in agreement. She was sure He would. But it would be such a relief to her mind to have it all neatly laid out before her. It was very hard to take it one step at a time.

Her mother phoned. "We were wondering if you'll be

able to come home for Easter. It seems such a long time since we've seen you. Henry can't get away. That new officer is still taking some watching. Henry says Maurice rather loses patience with him at times."

"Henry says Milton—that's his name, Milton Furbridge—is a bit lacking in police sense. I had to check with your father on that one. He says some people have a natural ability to know what should be done and how and when. In police work that is important—and it makes it so much easier for all concerned. Others have to learn it the hard way. 'Always bumping their noses against the grid,' was how your father put it. Anyway, Henry says it is much too far to travel for such a short time.

"I thought maybe you could come, dear. Doesn't take long to come up on the train. Then catch a ride out with Mr. Carson. You do get a long weekend, don't you?"

"I've a better idea," Christine suggested. "Why don't you and Dad come down? He gets a long weekend, too, doesn't he? You could come on the train, and maybe Henry and Amber could drive up here. At least for Easter Sunday."

There was silence.

"I'll have to talk to your father," Elizabeth finally said. But Christine could tell that her mother was excited about the idea. "You're sure it's okay with your aunt Mary?" she asked.

"It was her idea. Just the other day. 'Wouldn't it be fun if they could come?' Aunt Mary said. 'Maybe Henry and that other boy could meet your folks here,' she said."

"What other boy? Danny?"

"No. I think she meant Maurice Laray."

"Oh, wouldn't that be nice? But he couldn't. They'd never be able to leave Milton on his own," Elizabeth concluded. Christine wasn't sure if she felt disappointed or relieved about that part of the plan.

"I'll talk to your father," her mother was saying again.

"It would be wonderful if we could work it out."

When Christine hung up the phone, she turned to her aunt. "I think they'll come," she said, excitement edging her voice. "Mama said she'll have to talk to Dad, but I could tell she was ready to do some convincing. Unless something happens that he can't leave, I think they'll come."

"Good," said Mary. "I don't know when we've had a chance to have Easter together. See. That's another advantage in having you here."

Christine was already mentally planning all the things she wanted to do with her folks. She'd take them to the canteen one evening and let them see firsthand the work that was being done with the young service personnel. She'd bring them by the building that housed her new job. She'd even give them a peek into her bankbook to let them know she was not squandering her paychecks.

It would be so good to have a nice long visit again instead of hurrying through costly phone calls.

"Oh, I do hope they'll come," she explained, kissing her aunt on the cheek. "Thank you for saying we could invite them."

Mary laughed. "My dear girl," she said, "your parents are always more than welcome in our home. They aren't able to visit nearly often enough. We'll make a great celebration of it. Have all the kids home to join us. I'll get Lucy working on the plans right away."

Chapter Thirteen

When the word came that her folks were planning to come for the long Easter weekend, Christine began to count the days. And when Henry phoned that they would meet the family in Calgary, her excitement was nearly more than she could contain.

Her aunt Mary seemed to be almost as enthusiastic as she was. "Do you realize we have never had our two families all together at the same time? Oh, William and his family must come, they just must."

And Mary promptly rang William in Winnipeg. Christine heard part of the conversation. "Your aunt Beth and uncle Wynn will be here, and Henry and Amber are coming too. You haven't met Henry's new wife yet. She's so sweet. You haven't been home for just ages. I've missed the little ones so." She caught herself. "Oh, I've missed you and Violet, too, of course—but the little ones change so much in such a short time. I hate to miss all of that. Oh—bless them. Oh—that's sweet."

A long pause while William must have been talking.

"Yes. Yes—of course we understand. But if it works out,

we'd so love to have you. Where will we put everyone? I've got all these extra rooms. Yes, Christine is with us. I don't know how we would have made out without her help. Yes. I expect they will stay with us. I know. I know how many children you have. But the girls are here. They'd love to share rooms with family. Their children would be so excited to have their cousins. I know. I know it's a busy time. But it would be such a wonderful opportunity to all be together. We never have, you know. I know, dear. Well, you do what you think is best. Give my love to Violet and the kids. Yes. Yes, you too. Bye-bye."

Christine heard the soft click of the receiver. Her aunt reentered the room, running her hands over her skirts in nervous excitement. Her eyes were sparkling. "I think they'll come," she said. Christine smiled and wondered what had happened to *"You do what you think is best."*

"He says he is very busy in the office right now, but he will try to clear things so they can come. He says the kids have been begging to go to Nana's house. Isn't that sweet? My, I miss them."

Later that evening William called back to say they were making plans to come. Christine had never seen her aunt Mary so animated. Mary immediately began telephoning her daughters. "They're coming. We'll all be here. Oh, isn't it wonderful? It'll be like birthdays and Christmas all rolled into one."

One after another the calls were repeated to Sarah, Kathleen, and Lizbeth, each one with more excitement than the last. "We'll get together and make the plans. Work out the details. We'll have our Easter dinner here, of course. It will be so much fun to have to stretch out the table. I still haven't sat down and counted noses. Can you come over for coffee in the morning? We'll work it all out then."

Christine had to agree. It would be like one large Christmas and birthday celebration.

———

Wynn and Elizabeth would be the first to arrive. Wynn had arranged to take a few extra days in Calgary. He had some police business to attend to in the city and could do so while Elizabeth spent more time visiting. Christine rode with Jon and Mary to meet their train.

The conversation was lively on the way home. Elizabeth had to hear all the details about the coming weekend. "It will be so good to see William, Violet, and their little ones. I haven't seen them for ages," she enthused.

"His little ones aren't so little any more," Jonathan chuckled.

"My, no," added Mary. "Leticia is already fourteen. I can scarcely believe it. Brenda is ten and Mark is eight. And then they have the little tagalong. Paul Jonathan is only two."

They were speaking of family members Christine had never even met.

"They will be staying with Kathleen—except for Leticia. She will go to Tom and Sarah's. Sarah's Janet is about the same age. They write one another regularly. Janet spent a few weeks in Winnipeg last summer. Audrey doesn't think it fair that she doesn't have a girl cousin her age. 'Boys aren't much good as cousins,' she says. William's Mark and Kathleen's Toby are her age, but they are a little too rowdy for Audrey. And Mitchell is always busy trying to keep up with them even though he's only six. Of course Lizbeth's little Andrew is still much too young to attempt keeping up with the pack. He's not even walking yet."

"I do so look forward to seeing them all," Elizabeth said again.

"It's going to be fun," was the general consensus of everyone in the car.

———

It was raining when the train from the East pulled into the station. They all were gathered to meet it, young cousins dashing around excitedly calling to one another while parents tried to keep them firmly in control. Christine smiled. How did one ever harness so much exuberance? Even baby Andrew protested against being held, squirming to get down and crawl on the station floor.

At long last the whistle blew. They had to hold the children back to wait for the passengers to disembark, and then pandemonium broke out. Cousins greeted cousins with such wild excitement that Christine had to back up a few paces. She was concerned that the stationmaster might approach and ask them all to leave the premises. At length the greetings settled to a more normal level, and they busily sorted out passengers and luggage and prepared to load the vehicles for the trip back to Nana's house. A late evening meal had been planned for all to share together. Christine wondered just how things would be once the cousins were turned loose in the house.

But it was more controlled than she imagined it would be. The cousins seemed to break up in little groups by ages and go their separate ways, leaving the adults to try to catch their breath and get to know one another again.

After a few moments, the cousins were gathered once again and the meal served. The children ate much more quickly than the adults and, because of the circumstances, were excused early and allowed to go off to play once again. Only babies Andrew and Elizabeth, in their high chairs, and young Paul Jonathan, who had fallen asleep on his father's knee, were left.

The joyful chaos now turned into soft murmurs, punctuated by occasional laughter.

"When does Henry arrive?" William wanted to know.

"Tomorrow," answered Elizabeth. "He has to work until four o'clock and will drive up after that. He warned us that he won't be early. Said we should hang out the latchkey and all go to bed. I'm sure he knows better than that."

William smiled knowingly and joked, "So no one will see them until Saturday, then?" He laughed as Elizabeth tried to explain that she would be staying up until they arrived.

"You always were a tease, William," she said when she caught on.

"We're planning on a late breakfast here on Saturday morning," put in Mary. "We thought about nine o'clock if the children can last that long."

William nodded. "We'll give them a piece of toast if they're up too early."

Gradually the gathering broke up with many promises to one another about what the next day's activity would hold, but Christine paid little attention. She had to be in at the office. She felt a little cheated, not to be able to share the day. Being part of a large, close family reminded her of the feel in the Indian village where she had grown up. Like everyone belonged together. Looked out for one another. She had missed that.

The next evening they sat around and sipped coffee and ate chocolate cake while waiting for the hours to tick by. They were alone once again—just Jon and Mary, Wynn and Elizabeth and Christine. The others had all taken tired children to various homes to tuck them into bed. It had been a busy day—Christine wondered just who was more exhausted, the children or their parents.

Now it was quiet.

The evening was warm and pleasant, so they had not

built a fire in the hearth. Christine was well aware that one pair of eyes or another traveled often to the clock on the mantel as each person tracked the journey. If Henry got away promptly after four, and if they had no delays, ate a picnic lunch on the way, and did not stop long for a gas fill-up, they could arrive as early as ten o'clock. Perhaps even as early as nine-thirty if things went especially well.

At least the roads would be good. The rain had not lasted long. Just enough to settle the dust for good driving, her father had declared. The country roads could be rather nasty if they got either too dry or too wet.

"William has such a nice little family," Elizabeth was saying. "So well mannered. I have always appreciated good manners in a child."

Mary beamed her pleasure at the compliment about her grandchildren.

"They get a little rambunctious at times," Jonathan noted with a chuckle.

"They wouldn't be healthy children if they didn't," Mary defended stoutly.

They talked of many things. The clock ticked on. Nine-thirty came and went. There was no longer the possibility that the journey had gone better than hoped. Ten o'clock arrived. Still no sound of a car pulling up in the driveway.

Ten-fifteen. Elizabeth's eyes were constantly on the clock, her ears so attuned to the sound of a motor that she no doubt was missing much of the conversation.

Ten-thirty.

"Why don't you give Maurice a call and see if Henry was held up before getting away?" Elizabeth asked Wynn.

"I don't have his number. Besides, he may have retired by now."

"Well—just call the office, then. Someone will be working."

Wynn looked at the clock. "Let's give it another half hour or so," he suggested.

A quarter to eleven.

Christine felt herself yawn. It was getting late and she had been up early. Her mother must have seen her. "Why don't you go to bed, dear? You'll see them in the morning."

Then Elizabeth turned to Jon and Mary. "Why don't you go off to bed too? No need for us all to stay up and wait."

"I don't mind," said Mary.

"But it's getting so late. You must be worn out. You've had such a big day and tomorrow—"

"It's all right, Beth," Mary said as she stood and began to gather coffee cups on the tray. "I think I'll just slip out to the kitchen and wash up these things while we're waiting."

Christine stood, too, and stretched. "I'll help you," she offered, glad to have something to do to help pass the time. The conversation had lagged to almost a standstill.

They were in the kitchen for twenty minutes. Christine had listened for the sound of the front door opening, followed by excited greetings, but she had heard nothing.

By the time they returned to the living room, Elizabeth's face showed strain. It was now eleven fifteen. Without a word, Wynn rose from his chair and moved to the hall phone. It was some time before there was any sound from him.

"Larry? Oh—Officer Furbridge, sorry to bother you. This is Henry's father. Yes—here in Calgary. No—no. No problem. I just wondered if Henry was able to get away as he had planned. He was? Good. No. No, he hasn't arrived yet. No. I'm sure everything is fine. He may have had a bit of car trouble. Or some holdup. No—no, I didn't mean a holdup—just a delay. Some delay. Okay. Thank you. Yes. Thanks."

Christine was sure her mother had listened to the one-sided conversation with mixed emotions. Henry had left on time. That should be good news. But why had he not yet arrived? Her father had suggested car trouble. It was plausible. Cars were always breaking down at inconvenient times.

Maybe the roads. Just because Calgary had received only a light rainfall did not mean that other places had. It could have rained much harder in Henry's area. Maybe even caused a washout or trouble with a bridge—

"He would have called if—"

"He wouldn't have a phone," said Wynn before Elizabeth could finish.

"Surely he would have been able to find one—somewhere—by now."

"Maybe they decided to picnic on the way," suggested Jonathan. "Make a day of it. You know how Danny loves to fish. The time can sneak by when you're not watching."

"That isn't like Henry," murmured Elizabeth, visibly troubled.

"Why don't you go to bed?" offered Wynn. "No need for you to—"

"You know I'd never be able to sleep."

"Well, at least you could rest."

"No—I could not." The words were spoken rather sharply.

"I think I'll make us some tea," said Mary, rising to her feet.

"My word. We'll be waterlogged," murmured Elizabeth distractedly, but Mary left to make the tea regardless.

Christine crossed to the fireplace. She wished they had made a fire. At least the flames would be something to watch, something to draw their attention away from the worried expressions in each other's eyes. She squeezed at the back of her aching neck. Her eyes went again to the clock. Almost midnight. She agreed with her mother on one thing. It was not like Henry to keep them waiting without getting word to them—somehow. He would know their agitation and concern. It just wasn't like Henry.

And he would know that the latchkey would not be out. That they would all be sitting, waiting for their arrival.

She crossed to her mother. "Would you like me to rub your neck?" she asked, knowing how her own felt and that Elizabeth loved to have her neck massaged.

Her mother didn't even look up. "No," she said tersely, then seemed to catch herself, giving Christine a forced smile with an added, "Not now, thanks."

Christine withdrew.

Mary came with the tea. Everyone in the room accepted a cup, though no one seemed to pay any attention to its contents. They just sat holding it, absentmindedly watching the steam rise upward.

The phone rang and everyone in the room jumped. Jonathan was there in a few strides. "Yes. Yes. No—no, I'm afraid not. No. Very well."

"A wrong number," he said with a weary shrug. "Some guy's spent too long at the tavern."

Shoulders slumped with more fatigue.

Elizabeth set aside her cup and began to pace. "It's just not—something's not right," she said, blinking back nervous tears. "Henry wouldn't do this."

Wynn rose and pulled her close. He held her for a long moment before saying, "I think you're right, Elizabeth. Something must have happened that wasn't planned. It isn't like our son. I think we need to pray."

Gently he eased her to the couch and sat down beside her. She was freely weeping now. He handed her his pocket handkerchief and let her wipe her tears. Then he took her hand and started to pray. The other family members in the room drew near and reached out hands to join in a circle, heads bowed, and tear-filled eyes closed.

"Lord, you know our concern. You know the circumstances of our son and his family. Whatever those circumstances, we ask for your divine intervention on their behalf. Be with them, Lord, wherever they are. Meet any needs that they might have at this hour. Bring them to us—safely—quickly. Quiet our hearts and minds as we wait. We admit our dependence on you, God, our need for your presence and peace. We thank you that we can trust you with all things. In the name of Jesus, your Son, amen."

They looked up, drew gently apart, wiping tears from cheeks, blowing noses. Seeking to once again gain control of frayed emotions.

Christine saw the hands on the clock steadily ticking toward one in the morning.

"I think I'll take that shoulder rub now," her mother said with resolve. Christine moved forward to comply but was stopped by the sound of the doorbell. The entire room came alive.

"Thank you, Lord," Christine heard her mother murmur as she sprang from the couch and moved toward the hall. Wynn followed closely behind her, Christine a few steps back.

Her mother flung open the door, words of relieved greeting already beginning. "Henry—"

A uniformed police officer stood in the arc of porch light—but not their Henry. He reached up and awkwardly pulled off his billed cap.

"Mrs. Delaney?" he asked hesitantly, shifting from one foot to the other.

Wynn reached for Elizabeth and nodded at the man.

"I'm sorry to inform you . . . your son and family have been in a motor vehicle accident."

Christine saw her mother go limp in her father's arms.

Chapter Fourteen

Looking back on that night, it was hard to untangle the rest of the events. Somehow Christine and her folks got to the local hospital. Somehow they sorted through the scant details. Somehow they found themselves in Henry's room, looking down on the swollen, bandaged face of the man who was their son and brother. The doctor hovering nearby informed them in a low but professional voice that Henry "sustained a blow to the head that has resulted in a concussion. The prognosis is good. The X-rays indicate that he can be expected to regain consciousness without much delay and should have no significant future problem."

Sick with fear, Christine wondered just what that meant.

Elizabeth stood silently weeping beside Henry's bed, one hand lovingly stroking his exposed arm where the IV needle fed something into his bloodstream.

"How are the others?" Christine heard her father ask, his voice husky with emotion.

"His wife is resting comfortably. We've given the boy a

sedative to quiet him. He was understandably quite emotional."

"We need to see them," said Elizabeth, wiping her eyes. Christine was surprised at how brave and in control her mother had become.

"This way," said the doctor.

Amber's room was just down the hall. She, too, was swathed in bandages for the facial cuts the doctor told them about. She also had suffered a broken pelvis along with the cuts from flying glass. What they could see of Amber's face was pale, but she was conscious. She reached out a hand to them, and tears began to fill her eyes. Elizabeth leaned over and held her, and they wept together.

"How . . . how are they?" she asked, brokenly.

"Danny is . . . is resting. They've given him something to help him sleep. Henry . . . will be fine. He got a bump on the head and he was cut up a bit—but he'll be fine," Elizabeth tried to reassure her daughter-in-law.

"It happened so quickly," said Amber, staring vacantly at the ceiling.

"Just what happened?"

She shook her head. "I'm . . . I'm not really sure. We had just come into town—"

"You were in town—here?" Elizabeth sounded incredulous.

Amber nodded.

"We had arrived—shortly before ten, I think. Henry had . . . had just remarked that we'd made good time. We approached this intersection. Then I heard Henry say, 'Oh no,' or something like that, and when I looked up this car came smashing into us. I don't . . . I don't think I ever lost consciousness. I heard Danny screaming, but I couldn't see him. I reached for Henry, but he was . . . he was limp. Draped over the steering wheel. I was so frightened. I thought he was dead." Amber broke into sobs again while

Elizabeth patted her shoulder. She finally was able to continue. "And then people started to come, and everyone was yelling and running, and soon I heard sirens. I knew help was on the way.

"I was so thankful when I saw a man checking Henry and heard him say, 'He's still breathing,' but I was afraid he'd never make it to the hospital. There was blood all over and—"

"Shh," whispered Elizabeth, holding the girl again. "Don't talk about it. Try not to think about the accident. You're all safe now. It's going to be okay. Shh."

Wynn moved close to take Amber's hand while Christine stood back. Still. Mute. What was intended to be a great family celebration had turned into a tragic nightmare.

"I'm so worried," whispered Amber. "We thought we were bringing you good news—now I'm so frightened—"

"What do you mean?" Christine saw her mother's eyes wide with concern.

"We . . . wanted to tell you this together. We . . . we are going to have a baby."

Elizabeth gave a little gasp, then hugged Amber as close as she dared.

"We . . . we were so excited. Henry wanted to tell you himself. That was one reason we came now. But after . . . after this I'm afraid I might lose it." She was weeping again.

"Is the doctor aware—?" began Wynn, moving closer to the bed.

"Yes. Yes—I told him right away. He says they will do all they can, but the pelvis . . ." Amber blinked back tears.

Her injury suddenly had more significance.

"I was only eight weeks along. It's so early. I . . . I really am afraid that—"

"You try to rest," Elizabeth comforted, patting her daughter-in-law's arm. "We are going to see Danny—then we'll pop back in and sit with you."

Danny was sound asleep with the help of the sedative. His face had two cuts. Other than that, he looked whole. They each whispered prayers of thanks. He was being held for observation, the doctor had said. If all was as expected, he could be released sometime in the afternoon.

They went back to Amber's room. She seemed to have gotten herself well under control. Wynn left the women seated by her bed, telling them he would go out to the lobby to inform Jonathan and Mary of the situation. He soon was back with the two, and they made a brief tour to the three rooms and then were sent on their way home. There was nothing to be gained by them sitting out the night in the waiting room.

Then Wynn was gone again. At Elizabeth's questioning look, he had said something about looking into the police report. Christine was sure her father wanted to find out exactly what had happened. And why had it taken so long for the family to be notified.

By the time he returned, Amber had finally managed to fall asleep and seemed to be resting comfortably. Elizabeth looked about to fall asleep in her chair.

"I think it best we go home and try to get some rest," he advised. "We'll need to be back later. Danny will be waking, and perhaps Henry—"

"I want to look in on Henry before we leave," Elizabeth said quickly.

Wynn nodded.

With one last pat of Amber's hand, Elizabeth rose from her chair. They walked to Henry's room without conversation. He was just as they had left him. Christine noticed with thankfulness that his breathing sounded even. Elizabeth seemed to find it hard to leave the room. "Please be sure to call us the minute he awakens," she informed the nurse at the station desk. The woman simply nodded.

Christine wondered if anyone would be able to get any sleep.

———————

Word traveled quickly, and the family responded with shock and sorrow. The gathering became more like a somber funeral wake than the expected joyous reunion. Elizabeth gratefully accepted all their expressions of sympathy.

"Oh, Aunt Beth," said Kathleen, throwing her arms around her favorite aunt, tears on her cheeks. "I am so sorry."

Elizabeth returned the warm hug, holding Kathleen close for a long time. When she finally pushed back, she brushed at tears. But her countenance was remarkably controlled. "It could have been much worse," she said resolutely. "I feel our prayers were answered. God did protect them."

"Exactly what happened?" queried William.

"Some fellow ran a stop sign, Wynn found out from the police report. He'd had a bit too much to drink and said he didn't see it."

"And I suppose he walked away intact?"

"Not even a cut."

William shook his head.

"Hit them broadside on the passenger side," Wynn explained. "Amber got the worst of it. Henry struck his head. They're not sure on what. Danny was thrown around. He will be sore for a while, but nothing is broken." Wynn ran a hand over the back of his neck. He had told Christine privately that he would not relax until Henry was out of the coma—but he dared not let Elizabeth sense his agitation.

Elizabeth now forced a smile around the group. "We are going over to General Hospital, but why don't you just . . .

just try to have your party? It's not going to help for you all to be missing out on the fun of being together. Everyone is going to be okay. It will take a little time . . . but they'll make it. We have so much to be thankful for. So . . . go ahead. Enjoy your time together. That's the way Henry and Amber would want it."

It was a brave speech. Christine admired her mother and hoped the family members would be able to follow through with their plans.

The three headed back to the hospital as soon as they had downed some coffee. They didn't feel much like eating anything.

Just as they neared the desk a nurse looked up. "I was about to call you," she said. "I think your son is trying to wake up."

They hurried to Henry's room. The only indication that he was no longer in a deep sleep was an occasional groan and a movement of his head or hand. Wynn was the first to his side.

"Son. Son—can you hear me? We're here. Your mother and I and Christine. Can you open your eyes, Henry? Do you hear me, son?"

Elizabeth crowded in close and began entreaties of her own. "Henry? Dear? Can you hear us? We're here with you. Amber is okay. So is Danny. They are concerned about you. Are you awake?"

But Henry did not respond.

"I'm going to check on Amber and Danny," Christine whispered, partly because she could not stand to watch their seemingly futile attempts.

She found Amber still sleeping. The nurse leaving her room cautioned, "She needs to rest. That's the best thing for her right now."

Christine nodded. She would not awaken her sister-in-law.

She moved on to Danny's room. The little boy was just stirring. When he opened his eyes, he seemed totally confused. He looked about the strange room, then appeared greatly relieved when Christine came into his view.

"Where's my mom?" he asked immediately.

"She is here. She is still sleeping."

He looked puzzled. "Where is this? Is this Aunt Mary's house?"

"No. This . . . this is a hospital."

He pushed up from his pillow and grimaced. "Why did we come here?"

"Your mama and daddy are both here with you. There're just . . . just in another bedroom," said Christine, hoping to divert panic. She wasn't sure what to say to the child.

"Why?" he asked. "Why didn't we go to Aunt Mary's house?" There was fear in his eyes.

"Because," Christine said, struggling for words, "because your car was in an accident. You got some cuts that needed to be fixed."

"Did Mama get cuts too?" He put a hand to his face and felt the bandages.

"Yes. Yes—your mama got some cuts too."

He looked worried. "And Dad?"

"Yes—Dad too."

"Are they okay?"

"They're hurt right now—but they'll be okay."

"I hurt too."

"I know," said Christine, holding out her arms to him. He accepted the hug, clinging to her as she embraced him.

"Where are all the other people?" he asked, pulling away to look into her face.

"The other people?"

"The . . . Grandpa and Grandma and the . . . the cousins and stuff?"

"Well . . . Grandpa and Grandma are . . . are visiting your

daddy, and the cousins and stuff are at Aunt Mary's house."

"I want to visit my Daddy too."

"And you can. As soon as the doctor checks you—and says you can get out of bed. But your daddy is still very sleepy. He might not be awake."

"And Mama?"

"Your mama was sleeping, too, when I checked a minute ago. But I expect she will be waking up soon. Oh, look. Here's a book by your bed. Shall we read it?"

The boy was easily distracted as Christine began the story. She hoped the doctor would be around shortly. She didn't wish to try to answer more questions from little Danny.

———

When Danny was discharged that afternoon, Elizabeth sent Wynn and Christine out to purchase a new outfit for him. She did not want to worry him with the sight of his bloodstained garments. He seemed excited with the new clothes but puzzled about why he was leaving the hospital without his parents.

"We'll stop and see them on our way out," promised Christine.

True to her word, she took Danny first to his father's room. Danny wondered, "Why is he still asleep?" When there was no immediate answer, he continued. "Why has he got that thing poking him?"

"That's a special hospital needle. The doctor can give medicines with it."

"Why does he need medicines?"

Christine looked to her parents for help.

"You know how you felt when you were hurt?" asked Wynn. Danny nodded. "Well, your dad is hurting too. The medicine helps him get well."

"Why didn't they give me some?"

"Oh, they did. It was just a different kind. We have a little packet of pills to take with us to help you with your hurts."

Danny seemed satisfied. "Can I see Mom now?" he asked.

They exchanged glances, and then Christine hurried on ahead to make sure Amber was ready to see her son. Wynn and Elizabeth followed more slowly with Danny.

Christine could not believe how brave Amber was. In spite of her pain, in spite of her fears, she put on a smiling face and held out her hand to Danny.

"Danny. My, look at you. You are all dressed up."

"They got them for me," he said, grinning as he dipped his head in the direction of the other three.

"Well—you look so nice."

Danny was not to be sidetracked for long.

"Why are you in bed?"

Amber indicated that Danny should be boosted up to sit beside her, and Wynn lifted the boy. "Because I got a nasty bump in that accident."

"I see where your face got cut."

She nodded.

"I gots cuts too." He fingered the bandages. "But you got more."

"A few more. Cuts heal."

Danny nodded. "Where's your bump?"

"My leg. Not really my leg. Up here." She pointed out the spot.

"Does it hurt bad?"

She nodded. "It's broken."

His eyes widened. "Can they fix it?"

"Yes. But it will take some time. I have to stay in the hospital for a while."

He frowned.

"But you get to go home now. Well, not home—but to Aunt Mary's house with Auntie Christine. You get to see all of those cousins."

Danny looked unsure.

"When will you come?"

"Just as soon as I can."

That seemed to satisfy the boy. He gave his mother a good-bye hug and left with his grandfather and Aunt Christine. Elizabeth was returning to sit at the bedside of her son. She wanted to be there when he awakened.

"You're still worried, aren't you?" Christine asked her father in a low voice on the short drive to Jon's.

He merely nodded.

"Over her—or him?" She intended to speak vaguely so Danny, who was busy with a new toy car, would not be alarmed.

"Both . . . I guess. The leg will heal, but she could, well . . . you know."

Christine nodded to let him know she was following his thought.

"And him? The doctor said that he'll be fine once he—"

"They never know . . . for sure." Wynn's voice dropped to nearly a whisper, but not on account of Danny.

"So—"

"Don't say anything to your mother," Wynn said quickly. "It would just worry her needlessly. I trust the doctor is right—but the truth is, we won't know until he wakes up and responds."

Christine felt her stomach tighten. What if the doctor was wrong? What if Henry did not wake up? Or worse still, to her thinking, what if he awakened, but things were all wrong? What would it do to the entire family? The very thought made her feel sick inside.

———

Christine did not return to the hospital with her father. They all agreed that it was necessary for Danny to have someone near whom he knew. They need not have worried. His cousins all seemed excited about meeting him, and the boys near his age quickly had him involved in a game. Christine hoped that one of the children wouldn't inadvertently make a remark that would upset Danny, but the parents assured her that they had passed on as little information as possible. Anything the children knew Danny already knew himself. Christine tried to relax.

Her parents had promised to call the moment there was any change in Henry's condition. All through the day, Christine watched the clock. She knew those around her were trying valiantly to distract her—to involve her in conversation or activity, but she was unable to concentrate. Her thoughts were entirely on Henry and Amber. Was the baby still safe? Would Henry still be—be Henry when he finally awakened?

By late afternoon Kathleen approached her. "I think Danny is doing just fine with the kids. Would you like someone to drive you over to the hospital?"

Christine didn't trust herself to speak. She felt tears sting her eyes. "Please" was all she could whisper.

Frank acted as chauffeur. She thanked him sincerely and hurried in to find her parents. They were in Amber's room, offering consolation through their own grief. She had lost the baby after all.

With a sickness of soul Christine fled the room. She could not bear to hear the young woman's broken sobs.

She stumbled on to Henry's room. He was stirring in agitated fashion, but he still had not regained consciousness. Christine could not even bring herself to reach out to touch him. She stood back, watching his struggle for awareness. *Oh, Henry,* she cried silently, *when you do wake up—if you do wake up—who's going to tell you that you and Amber have just lost your child?*

The tears rolled down her cheeks, and she was well into her prayer before she even realized she was pouring out her sorrow and concern to her heavenly Father. What had she said to God? She wasn't sure. But He knew. He knew. He knew the cry of her heart.

Dear God, I love my brother, she continued through her tears. *I love him so much. He has been . . . been everything to me. Please . . . please let him be all right. Let him be . . . be Henry again.*

She could only wait and pray.

CHAPTER FIFTEEN

Christine finally found the courage to visit Amber later that evening. Amber's eyes were still red from her weeping, but she was now calm.

"I can hardly bear the thought of having to tell Henry that I have . . . have lost his child," she said. She picked listlessly at the edge of the white blanket as she lay against the pillow.

"It was your child too," Christine reminded her.

Amber nodded. "But Henry. He was so excited. He could hardly wait to tell you about it. He wanted to phone the very moment we were the least bit hopeful."

Christine almost said there would be more babies, but she caught herself. She knew that was not what Amber wished to hear at the present.

"He'll grieve," Christine said instead. "But much of his grief will be for you."

Amber blew her nose and took a shaky breath. Christine feared she had said the wrong thing. But when Amber lifted her eyes to Christine's, she even managed a weak smile. "I know he will. He is so sweet. So gentle and caring. I never thought I would be blessed with a man like him. I've been so . . . not lucky. I don't like that word. Blessed. Wonderfully blessed."

"And so has Henry," Christine stated, bringing a smile to Amber's pale face.

"You know . . ." Amber began, "I was a bit worried . . . at first. It seems silly now, but . . . Henry was so . . . so dedicated to you, to his parents, that I wondered if he could ever love me as much. But I needn't have worried. Henry has such a big heart. . . ." The rest was left unsaid. She started over. "I've no doubt that he loves me. He shows it a dozen times a day—in so many ways. He's a wonderful man, your big brother."

Christine could only nod, her eyes blurred with tears.

A stirring behind the curtain that divided the next bed from Amber's got their attention. Except for the coming and going of strangers visiting their family members, it was easy to forget there were other patients in the room. Christine tried not to be distracted by the intrusion. She turned back to Amber.

"I just wish I could be with him," Amber mourned. "It's so hard being apart."

Christine silently wondered how much comfort Amber would find in seeing Henry as he was now.

"Even if I could just see him. Know he's all right."

"He's not really all right . . . yet," Christine said carefully. "But the doctor assures us he will be."

"Yes . . . I know. They have promised to let me know the minute he wakes up. It seems like it's taking forever. If I could just speak to him, he might . . ."

"He might," agreed Christine.

They were quiet for many moments, each deep in thought.

"I worry about Danny. Does he understand what's happening?" Amber finally asked.

"We haven't told him any more than necessary. We don't want him to fret. He seemed fully involved in play when I left the house."

"Wasn't it gracious of God to arrange for all those cousins to be here just when Danny needed them?"

Christine had not thought of it that way. She had been thinking their plans had all been totally spoiled.

A nurse entered. "Mrs. Delaney. How are we doing? Have we been able to get any rest? It's time for another shot."

Why do they do that? Christine complained to herself. *Why do they always say "we" like they are actually part of it all? Well, perhaps that's the answer. Maybe they want the patient to feel they are in this together. They have a companion in their pain.*

"I think I'll slip back and check on Henry," Christine said, giving Amber's hand a squeeze. "I'll see you later."

There had been no change in her brother's condition that Christine could see. Wynn and Elizabeth still talked to him, still touched him, still coaxed him for some response, but there was nothing. Just the occasional fidget or moan.

"Why don't you go on back to Aunt Mary's and have something to eat and check on Danny?" Christine suggested. "Then I'll take a break when you come back."

"You're right," her father agreed, standing up. "If this is going to take a while, we should work out some kind of system. No one can be on duty twenty-four hours a day."

Elizabeth looked reluctant, but when Wynn brought her coat to her, she did not argue.

Christine settled in the chair by the bed and took Henry's hand. "Hey... wake up," she said, trying to keep her voice even. "Enough sleep. Open your eyes. Blink. Squeeze my hand. Do something."

She squeezed his hand. There was no response.

"Good evening."

The voice and the step brought Christine's head

around. A man in a white lab coat, a hospital chart-board in his hand, stood in the doorway.

"I'm Dr. Carlton," he said, moving toward the bed. "And you are. . . ?"

"Christine. Christine Delaney."

"His sister?"

"Yes."

"Sorry to meet you under such unpleasant circumstances, Miss Delaney," he said, shaking her hand. He sounded sincere. "It was nice to hear that the little boy was discharged. Danny, isn't it?"

"Yes," said Christine again.

Christine stood and moved her chair so the doctor had free access to the bed. He worked quickly, checking instruments and charts and talking to Henry the entire time as though the man was fully awake.

"Your wife, Amber, is doing fine, Henry, but she is anxious to see you. And Danny has gone on to Grandma's house."

Christine did not attempt to correct him. There was no need for him to try to untangle the gaggle of relatives who had gathered for the weekend.

"Now we just need to get you going again, Henry. Can you open your eyes for me? Think, Henry. Concentrate hard. Can you open your eyes? Can you squeeze my hand? What about the other one? Squeeze."

"Has he been doing anything?" the doctor asked Christine when there was no visible response. "Have you seen his eyes blink? Move at all?"

"He does move a bit . . . at times. Just . . . just his left hand and . . . and his head some. And he sort of moans. Not words really."

"That's encouraging," the doctor nodded.

Christine could find little encouragement in the feeble description she had just reported.

"At least something is going on in there." The doctor made some notations on his pad. "The nurses will soon be in to bathe him and change his bed linen."

Christine assumed this was a polite invitation for her to leave the room.

"I'll go visit my sister-in-law," she said, moving toward the door.

"I just came from there. She's sleeping."

"Oh. Well . . . I'll go on down to the lobby, then."

"There's a small room for family members right down the hall. Has anyone shown it to you?"

Christine shook her head.

"It's a bit more relaxing and private than the lobby. Third door on the right. Just walk in."

He was still writing notes on his chart. Christine murmured her thanks and left.

Third door on the right. It wasn't at all hard to find. She was relieved to discover the room was vacant. She took a seat by the one window and laid her head back. She was so weary. So very weary and a long night stretched before them. Was Henry ever going to wake up?

She closed her eyes. Only then did she realize that soft music was coming from somewhere. It was a simple hymn. She knew it. She groped around mentally to find the words. When the song reached the chorus, she followed along silently.

Count your blessings, Name them one by one.
Count your blessings, See what God hath done.
Count your blessings, Name them one by one
Count your many blessings, See what God hath done.

Christine let the words wash over her soul. If she were to start to count, just how many would be on her list? She hadn't been counting blessings. She had been counting woes—but surely . . .

They were all alive—Henry, Amber, and Danny.

They were in a hospital where they could get care.

There could be more babies—painful as the loss was now.

They had family members who loved them and shared their concern.

They were still in God's hands.

Someone at the door brought Christine's head up. "You found it," the doctor said with a smile. "Good. Here—I brought you a coffee. I don't know how you take it, but it being hospital coffee, I figured it would need all the help I could give it. I put in both cream and sugar. I found a few stale cookies too."

In spite of herself, Christine smiled. "Thank you," she said, accepting the cup. "I'll have to add that to my list."

"List?"

"I was just sitting here counting my blessings," she said, with a slight wave toward the corner radio that continued to play.

"That's a great exercise for all of us."

"It is," she replied. "One I had temporarily neglected."

"You've had a lot on your mind," he said.

Christine took a sip of the coffee. She didn't normally use sugar, but it was hot and strangely comforting.

"Just how is he?" she asked frankly.

The young doctor shook his head. "These things are so hard to read. It looks like everything should be okay." He hesitated, deep in thought. "But I wouldn't stop praying yet," he said just as frankly.

"So . . . there is a chance that . . . that he could be more seriously—"

"There's always a chance. We can never be one-hundred percent sure. The X-ray looks good. Let's hang on to that." He smiled.

The music switched to "What a Friend We Have in Jesus."

"Here, have a cookie."

He pulled a white napkin from his breast pocket and unwrapped two cookies. "I'm not sure if the cookies are supposed to take away the taste of the coffee or if the coffee is to wash down the cookies—but it was the best I could do."

With a smile Christine accepted a cookie.

"Are you from out of town too? I understand your brother was just coming into town."

"That's right. But I'm ... well ... I'm not quite sure where I'm from right now."

His eyebrow lifted.

"My folks are at Athabasca."

"Your dad's a cop, too, I understand."

"RCMP. Yes."

"Does he not like being called a cop?"

Christine shrugged. "I've never heard him say. But my mother doesn't care for the term."

"I'll keep that in mind." He grinned. "But you're not living at home, I take it."

"No. No, I've been working here in the city."

"Here?" His eyebrow rose again. "So where do you work?"

Christine told him.

"And you live...?"

Christine explained about coming to help Aunt Mary and staying on as a boarder.

"And if I'm not being too bold, what else do you do— besides work?"

"I ... I help out at the Hope Canteen ... as a volunteer."

"I've heard of it. It sounds like a great ministry."

"And I go to church."

"I've never seen you at mine." She could tell he was teasing.

"And yours is?"

"Community Fellowship."

"No . . . no, I've never been there. I attend a mission on Third Street with my aunt and uncle."

"Small?"

"It was. It isn't small anymore. They are planning to build."

"That's good."

He finished his coffee and stood. "By the way, I poked my head into your sister-in-law's room on my way by. She's awake now."

Christine rose as well. "Thank you. I'll . . . I'll go right in."

He nodded and held the door. "You may use this room anytime," he told her. "It's here for the families of our patients."

"Thank you," she said again. Then added, "And thank you for the coffee—and cookie too. It was—"

"Don't say delicious," he joked.

"I was going to say 'very thoughtful.' I appreciated it."

He nodded and was gone.

When Christine reached Amber's room, she found that her father and mother had returned. "I was about to send your father out to look for you," Elizabeth said.

"There's a room. Right down the hall. They were bathing Henry, and Amber was sleeping, so I—"

"Good," said Wynn. "I'm glad you got a little rest. Were you able to nap?"

Christine did not say she'd had a relaxing conversation with one of the hospital doctors. "No. I had a cup of coffee."

Amber looked much brighter, her eyes clearer, since her rest. Christine exchanged relieved glances with her mother.

"A nurse is in with Henry now," her father said. "They are giving him another dose of medicine. She said she will just be a minute."

"I think your father should drive you home now," said Elizabeth. "It's your turn for a break."

Christine was surprised at how tired she felt. The cup of coffee and cookie had mostly served to remind her of how hungry she was.

"I think I would like that," she agreed.

She kissed her mother good-night and looked in on Henry one last time. The nurse was still fussing with the IV. Then Christine turned and followed her father out to the car.

"I think Danny would like you to tuck him in—if he's not already asleep by the time you get there. He just had his pill before we left the house. I've no idea if it is a sedative as well as painkiller, but if it is, he's probably sleeping by now."

"I'll check."

"Don't think about coming back tonight," Wynn told her. "You need to get some rest."

"You're not planning to stay all night, are you?"

"I'm not sure I can get your mother away. Perhaps we'll make use of that room you spoke of. Does it have a couch where she could lie down?"

"I didn't even notice. I sat in a chair. But it was comfortable."

They drove up in front of Jon's. Christine reached for the car door handle. "Dad," she said, turning back to him. "What happens if . . . if Henry doesn't make it?"

"We've no reason to think he won't make it," he said, almost too quickly.

"But, what happens if . . . if he doesn't get better? Can't work anymore?" The words scarcely could make it passed the lump in her throat.

"I don't know," he said honestly. "We'll just have to take it as it comes."

"He'd hate that—not being a cop." She used the term in spite of her mother. "That's the only thing he's ever wanted to be."

"I know."

She opened the door and slid out. The evening was still warm. She turned to watch her father drive away. She had almost forgotten—tomorrow was Easter Sunday. A day of new beginnings. A day of hope—of resurrection. A day of celebration. She wondered what the day would hold for them.

———

It was only the flicker of an eyelid at first. They almost missed seeing it. When it didn't occur again, they thought perhaps it had been imagined. Then a finger twitched. Once—then twice. It was another fifteen minutes before Henry's eyes opened partially. But they closed again, and despite their urgent coaxing, they did not reopen.

Elizabeth took the limp hand in both of her own. "Son. Son, listen to me. Son, can you hear me? Squeeze my hand. Squeeze, Henry."

Suddenly her eyes widened, staring in shock. "He did," she gasped. "He squeezed."

"Do it again," suggested Wynn. Christine knew her father thought it might merely be an involuntary reaction. Wynn leaned over the hand and watched carefully as Elizabeth repeated her command.

"Squeeze my hand, Henry. Squeeze it, son," she implored as only a mother could.

The fingers visibly tightened around Elizabeth's. "He did. He did," cried Christine as Wynn broke out in a broad smile.

"Ring for the nurse," Wynn instructed her. Elizabeth was far too engaged with talking to her son.

"Henry—we've been so worried," Elizabeth said. "Open your eyes, son. Talk to us. We're here, Henry. We're right here. Talk to us, son. Can you open your eyes?"

Henry did.

At first they looked vacant, seeming not to focus on anything in the room. In response to the call, a nurse rushed through the door, followed quickly by two doctors. But Elizabeth refused to give up her spot, even for the medical personnel.

"It's me, Henry. Your mother. Can you speak to us?"

Henry's head moved slightly as though to clear his vision. He still looked confused. His eyes turned toward Elizabeth. He frowned.

"It's me, Henry," Elizabeth said again.

"Mother. Where am I?" were his first words, sounding husky but clear—words that brought the two doctors in closer to his bed.

"Henry," said the older one. "Henry, how do you feel?"

"What happened?" asked Henry.

"You were in a bit of an accident. Took a bump on the head."

Henry struggled to lift his head. "Amber? Is she—?"

"She's fine. And so is that boy of yours."

"Danny."

"Yes, Danny. He's already been discharged."

Henry settled back against his pillow and closed his eyes again. Elizabeth leaned forward anxiously, but a doctor's gentle hand restrained her.

"He must rest," he advised, and she relaxed.

He nodded toward the door, and the group followed him. The other doctor remained behind, checking heart rate and writing notes on his pad.

"That's good—very good—for a start." The doctor

seemed genuinely pleased. "He recognized you and he re-membered his family. That's a positive sign."

"Now what?" from Wynn.

"We can only wait and see. Next time he wakes up, I expect him to be much more alert. Remember, as well as the concussion, he has also been on medication to help him rest so the healing can take place. I think we can start to ease off on that now."

"How long?"

"What I suggest is that you all go home and get a good night's sleep. We'll see what tomorrow holds. We want Henry to get undisturbed sleep himself tonight."

"But what if he wakens and asks for us?" Christine could tell her mother could not imagine not being there.

"I think we'll keep him asleep tonight."

"We must go see Amber," Wynn prompted. "She'll want to know all about—"

"Yes." Elizabeth turned to head for Amber's room. "We have such good news to share."

But was it actually good news? Christine wasn't sure. There hadn't been time to bring Amber to Henry's hospital bed before he had slipped back into unconsciousness again. But he had, for those brief minutes, been able to remem-ber—able to reason. Perhaps that would be enough to give Amber hope.

Christine followed her folks from the room. She thought of the morning service in the little church where they had all worshiped together before coming to the hos-pital. There had been earnest prayer as the congregation knelt together. "Lord, on this Easter Sunday of deliverance and restoration, we ask for another miracle from your hand," the minister had prayed. "If it is your will, place your healing touch on Henry. Touch his body and his mind. Bring him back to his family, Lord, we pray."

It seemed that their prayers were beginning to be an-swered.

Chapter Sixteen

There are all sorts . . . of pieces missing."

Henry's progress had seemed awfully slow to Christine, but he was gradually looking and sounding more like himself. He was allowed wheelchair visits to see Amber and was now able to do most things for himself. The doctors were even speaking of discharge.

But Christine could tell he was worried.

"It takes time," she tried to reassure him. "The doctors all say—"

"I know what the doctors say. But some of the fog should have cleared by now."

"Much of the fog has. Think back. Even in the past few days you have improved tremendously." She was talking to herself as much as to her brother.

He grinned wryly. "I appreciate your attempt to humor me—but I'd be careful how I use the word 'tremendously.'"

"You do admit there has been improvement?"

Henry nodded.

"Well . . . to my way of thinking . . . any improvement is tremendous."

"Okay. All right," he said with a chuckle. Then he sobered. "But I'm ready for a lot more tremendous improvement. It's just not happening fast enough, Chrissy."

Her eyes dropped to her hands that held the magazine she had been perusing. "I wish I could . . . do something."

"Hey," he responded, reaching out to lift her chin like he had often done over the years when they were growing up and she was sulking or feeling down. "You *are* doing something. Just being here—encouraging and cheering me on—that's doing something. Far more than you might realize." Before Christine could even respond, he went on, "And looking after Danny for us—that's doing something."

"The truth is, it's Aunt Mary who is doing most of the looking after Danny—and loving every minute of it."

"It makes Amber feel so much better knowing he is happy and busy—and loved."

Christine nodded and smiled, thinking about how quickly this little boy had made his own place in their family.

"This has been really tough for Amber," Henry noted soberly. "She feels so bad about losing the baby. I worry that she feels . . . feels almost guilty about it."

"It certainly wasn't her fault."

"No . . . no, but there's some . . . some strange . . . I don't know. I don't really understand it. But . . . well . . . a woman sort of sees her body as the . . . the protected dwelling of her unborn child. She . . . she nurtures and loves and helps it to grow and become . . . someone . . . a person. When something goes wrong, she feels she has somehow failed. Failed to be the protector she was meant to be. It's hard for Amber. It's hard for me too.

"I already loved that child," Henry went on, gazing out the hospital room window. "I wanted him . . . or her . . . just as much as Amber did. But there's a difference, someway. I don't feel guilty—just angry. Angry at that driver who drank too much and dared to get behind the steering wheel. To take another life even before it had a chance to fully live. To injure and maim and cause total disruption of lives. To bring pain and concern to many more people than were in the car he hit."

Christine could see that Henry was getting upset. She reached out a restraining hand. "Don't think about it. Try not—"

"How can I not think about it?" Henry stared into Christine's face. "My son is being taken care of by others in a home not his own. My wife is lying with a broken pelvis and an even more painful broken heart. I don't know if I'll ever be able to work again, Christine. Maybe I'll just be a . . . a useless lump for the rest of my days. I wasn't on the job, so there won't be compensation for my wife and family. I—"

"Henry—don't," she begged him, tears beginning to run down her cheeks. "Please, don't. This . . . this doesn't help. . . ."

He leaned back on his pillow and closed his eyes. Christine could see his jaw working and knew he was struggling with his anger. She did not speak. What could she say?

Many minutes passed in silence. Christine closed her eyes as well and leaned her head back on the tall chair. It had been a horrendous time—for all of them. Henry was right. One man's carelessness had certainly brought pain to many people. The planned family celebration had never transpired. Her folks finally had taken the train back home, once the danger was passed. Her father was needed at his post, and Christine gathered that her mother insisted on going along simply because she could not bear to be separated from him at a time when she leaned on his strength. So now it was Christine who made the daily treks to the hospital after her day's work was done. She had not even been to Hope Canteen since the accident. She missed it, and she thought they might be missing her.

At length she opened her eyes again, but she did not lift her head. "Last week—when we were terribly concerned that you . . . that you might not come out of your coma, I was in this little room . . . just down the hall. As I sat there, a radio in the room was playing. I don't know the program. It was all hymns. Just one after the other, played on a piano. I was feeling . . . really down, and then I recognized the hymn being played."

She lifted her head so she could watch Henry's pale face, now tight with emotion.

"The song was 'Count Your Blessings.' At first I didn't even think I had any to count, and then I got to thinking of . . . of how much worse things could have been. I started to count. I really did—and like the song says, it surprised me. We do have things to be thankful for, Henry."

His nod was barely visible.

"Then this doctor—Dr. Carlton, I think he said his name was—suddenly appeared with a cup of coffee—really awful coffee." Christine managed a smile. "And a stale cookie. And I added that to my list. Oh, not the coffee and cookie—but the understanding. The reaching out of someone."

Henry's jaw had relaxed.

"It gave me a lift—it really did."

"Dr. Carlton?" Henry asked.

"I think that's his name."

"Yes, I know him. He's a good man. He's given me a lift, too, on more than one occasion."

Christine rubbed her hands together, wondering if she dared to speak further. At last she swallowed and plunged on. "Aunt Mary and I were talking a short time ago. About her fall—and all. And about the verse that says, 'All things work together for good.' Well, she said she didn't see her fall as God's doing or part of His plan or anything like that.

But she did see good that came later—good that maybe wouldn't have happened if she hadn't fallen and gotten hurt."

"So you're saying I should see this as some kind of good?"

"No. No, I'm not saying that at all. I'm just . . . I'm just trying to say that . . . even *in this*, God can make something good result—if we let Him."

She heard Henry's deep sigh. When she looked at him she noticed tears had squeezed out from under his closed eyes and were sliding down his white cheeks. "I needed that," he said in a half whisper. That was all.

Henry was discharged first. Because of the circumstances, the RCMP headquarters allowed him to stay in Calgary to be near his wife and further medical treatment if necessary. Christine thought each day he was remembering more of the missing pieces of his life, but she wasn't sure. Perhaps he was just very good at bluffing.

Much of his time was spent at Amber's bedside. The doctors seemed pleased with the progress of the healing bone, and gradually she was working through her grief as well.

Christine went to the hospital after work to be with Amber, and Henry and Danny spent that time in the evening together. Danny was not allowed hospital visiting privileges, so little exchanges were carried back and forth. Christine was sure an actual visit would have been beneficial to all, but rules were rules.

She was just leaving one evening when she nearly collided with a hurrying doctor in a white coat. While both were apologizing, Christine realized it was Dr. Carlton. When he recognized Christine, he smiled.

"I'm so sorry," he said again. "Most of the staff have learned to get out of the way when they see me coming. I have this bad habit of being totally preoccupied."

Christine returned his smile.

"You wouldn't have time for a cup of *great* coffee, would you?"

"The visiting-hour bell has already rung," she answered.

"Oh, that. Yes, well, that rings to clear the rooms so the nurses can prepare the patients for the night. It has nothing to do with the visitor's room."

Christine tipped her head slightly, sure that the bell meant visitors were to leave the hospital premises.

"The cafeteria? No one gets tossed out of the cafeteria."

Christine had to smile again.

"I'd really like to hear more about Hope Canteen."

"I . . . I haven't been able to get there lately."

"No—I wouldn't imagine." Somehow they had fallen into step and were heading toward the cafeteria. "Instead of helping others to prepare for battle, you've had a battle of your own to work through."

Christine nodded.

"How is Henry since his discharge?"

"I don't know," Christine admitted after giving her answer some careful thought. "At times, I think just fine. And then he . . . he hits a mood. Henry was never moody. Never."

"It's not unexpected." He sounded all doctor now. "Many people with Henry's type of trauma go through that emotional crisis."

Christine was alarmed. They had not been told. "Will it go away?" she asked.

"Usually. Almost always, in fact. But it takes time. Henry took quite a blow to the head. Brain bruise, we call it. There's a much more technical term, but folks get the idea when we call it brain bruise."

Christine nodded. She did get somewhat of a mental image of the injury.

"How long—?"

"We can never say. It depends on so many factors."

They had reached the cafeteria door, and he held it for her.

"The coffee here is a shade better than it is upstairs. But you might like to try the tea."

"Actually, I was thinking of something cold. Maybe a cola."

"Cola sounds good."

He held her chair while she settled at the small table, then ordered two colas from the young waitress in the striped apron and stiff cap.

"Your folks have left the city?" he asked as the young woman—"Molly" from her name tag—placed the frosty glasses in front of them.

"Yes. They went home last Thursday. Dad had to get back to work. He suggested that Mom stay—but she surprised me. She insisted on going home. I guess that means her mind is quite a bit more at ease about Henry."

"Mrs. Delaney seems to be doing well."

"Amber? Yes. She was quite cheerful tonight. Counting the days until she is able to be released."

"I can't understand it," he said, throwing up a hand in mock distress. "Here we take such good care of them. Bring them breakfast in bed every morning, rub their backs every night, wait on them hand and foot—and they still can't wait to check out of our hospital."

Christine sensed his light banter was meant to help her relax.

"Except one dear old soul," he chuckled. "We had to practically push her out the door, and every time we turned around she was back in again. Her shoulder ached or her toe hurt—anything. Anything at all. I was told she kept her hospital suitcase packed so she'd be all ready to go should she feel a twinge. Dear Miss Ache-a-lot."

"That was her name?"

"No—not officially."

Christine laughed.

He placed his elbows on the table and leaned forward. "Tell me about Hope Canteen."

"I haven't been there for so long I feel out of touch," she admitted.

"Almost two weeks," he said. "Two weeks tomorrow."

She was surprised.

"I've gone a couple times. Wanted to see it for myself. It's quite a place. They told me they miss you."

Christine felt her cheeks flush.

"Do you think you can make it back before too long?"

"I . . . I hope so. Henry spends the days with Amber, but he . . . he likes to have time with Danny in the evenings. So I visit the hospital then. Not that I wouldn't anyway," she hastened to add.

She toyed with the glass in her hand. "It's just . . . well, everything has been so . . . so disrupted. Sort of . . . fallen out of routine. It's hard to get back in step again."

He nodded.

"They have a batch of fresh recruits who are regulars now," he informed her.

"They do?"

"Fresh off the farms. And city streets, too, I would imagine. Just kids."

"Yes. I know."

"Some of them look scared. The cocky ones might be scared, too, but their bluff is better."

Christine shook her head. "It's the really young ones that bother me. Sending them off to war like that."

"I think the day will come when we'll look back and realize just how much we owe them." His words were solemn.

"I wish the war was over. I wish . . . I'm so afraid—they won't come back."

She was glad he didn't try to reassure her with empty,

foolish words. They both knew many of the young soldiers would not be coming back. The grim reality of war meant someone's husband, someone's brother would shortly leave the shores of Canada for the last time.

"Another cola?" he asked.

Christine stirred. "No. Thank you. I must be getting home."

She stood and he stood along with her.

"I plan on going again whenever I can find the time," he said softly. It almost sounded like an invitation for her to join him.

"I hope to go back, too, when things . . ."

"Don't wait too long. They need you." He smiled. Christine gave a little nod and gathered her purse.

———

At long last, Amber was discharged and brought to Jon and Mary's house by a relieved Henry and exultant Danny. "Look," he cried before he was even in the door. "My mom is here."

Amber was helped in and led to the couch in the living room. "I'm absolutely hopeless on crutches," she admitted with a laugh. "I just can't seem to find the right rhythm."

"There is no right rhythm for crutches," Mary responded. "I'm quite convinced of that."

They celebrated by making ice cream, which they ate with canned strawberries and chocolate sauce. It was still too early for fresh strawberries from the back garden.

"This is the best I ever tasted," Danny announced. Christine was sure that even spinach would have tasted good to the youngster in his excitement. "Are we going home now, Dad?"

"Maybe tomorrow," Henry smiled. "We'll see."

Henry had a visit to make to the local RCMP office the

next morning. After consultations with his doctors, they would decide what would be done with Henry. Christine knew Henry was undoubtedly anxious. She prayed inwardly that things might go well.

Amber retired early after her exhausting day. Christine was sure they were all feeling it. She would have liked to slip off to her room as well, but she did not want to leave Henry all alone. Mary and Jon had left for a meeting at the church.

"Amber is looking much better," she noted as they settled in the living room after tucking Danny in.

Henry nodded. "I think she finally has accepted the loss of our child. Pastor Blessing—isn't that an interesting name for a pastor—has called on her a number of times. It has helped."

"She told me."

"For one thing, he told her the baby could have been severely damaged by the accident. It was much kinder of God to take the little one home than for the baby to suffer with some awful handicap."

"Do you believe that?"

"What? That the baby could have been injured? Of course."

"That it was kinder to take it?"

Henry shook his head. "I'm not sure. Amber and I would have loved and accepted him—or her—regardless. As to the handicap bringing suffering—it depends. Many handicapped people live a full, rich life. I wouldn't take that away from them. We just don't understand their world, that's all."

"There's a young man who helps at Hope Canteen. He . . . has Down syndrome, I guess . . . but he . . . he's always happy. He pours coffee and passes out sandwiches, and everywhere he goes he is grinning and calling out to people. I sometimes think he brings more joy to others than any of the rest of us do."

"I guess it would depend on whether the handicap also brought unbearable pain."

"Yes—but even then, how do we know if the joy of just being alive—of interacting with others—outweighs the pain?"

"I'm glad the decision is not mine—but God's."

Christine let the minutes tick by.

"I met that young doctor again. Did I tell you?" she said eventually.

"Eric Carlton?"

"Eric? Is that his name? Well, I literally bumped into him at the hospital. We had a cola. He's been going to Hope Canteen some. He's as disturbed over all those young people going off to war as I am."

"They're not all young, you know. Many husbands and fathers are also—"

"I know. But it is basically the young ones whom we see at the canteen. They are the ones who are looking for some way to fill their evenings. Something to distract their attention."

"I'm glad he's going over there. He should be good with them."

"Yes. I think so. He said—perhaps it was just meant as an encouragement—but he said they are missing me."

"I'm sure they are." Henry stretched out long legs and leaned back. "Well, your life should soon be able to return to normal."

"And yours?"

"It depends what they say tomorrow. I do feel a bit better about it all. I seem to be able to concentrate better, and I don't . . . well, I've been able, with God's help, to work through the anger. I must admit I still worry some. If I'm not seen to be fit for work, I'm not sure what we'll do. I sure wouldn't want Amber to have to support the family by cutting hair all her life."

"Oh, Henry—it won't come to that."

He smiled but it looked a bit crooked. "Well, whatever comes, I have finally been able to leave it in God's hands. I love my work—you know that. But if I am not considered fit enough to continue, I'm sure God, as you said, can work out some good. At least I still have my wife and son. After an auto accident like we had, I am truly blessed."

The chorus of the song started through Christine's mind once more.

"You know, Chrissy," Henry went on quietly, "if I am allowed to continue with the RCMP, I'm not sure how I will ever handle it if I have to walk up to some door and inform parents—or a wife, or husband—that someone they love has just been killed or badly injured. I had to give that awful message to Amber those many years ago. I thought I had empathy then, but being through the accident myself, I know what devastation it brings to so many lives."

"If that time comes, you'll find the strength. He'll give it to you."

"He'll have to. I'll not be able to handle it on my own."

CHAPTER SEVENTEEN

The warm June evening did not call for the sweater Christine carried on her arm. But she was bringing it along to the service center to please Aunt Mary, who had suggested she might need it later. Life had indeed returned to normal. Henry and Amber and Danny were back in their own home. Henry was assessed to be physically and mentally fit, and he had been allowed to resume his policing duties. A new officer replaced Milton. The young man decided the RCMP hadn't turned out to be what he had imagined after all. He joined the RAF and was supposedly on his way to Britain to help rout the Nazis. Laray had been given a promotion for his handling of the office in the absence of Henry. Christine was pleased for Laray. But she pushed thoughts of him aside as she reached for the door handle.

"I shouldn't be too late," she called to her aunt.

"Have a good evening, dear," Mary responded just as the hall phone rang.

"Do you want me to get it? I'm still right here," Christine called again.

"Please, dear."

Christine lifted the receiver, hoping to hear her mother's voice. "Hello."

"Hello. Miss Delaney?"

"Yes?" Christine was hesitant.

"This is Eric Carlton. Remember me? The cola and coffee guy?" There was teasing in his voice.

"Of course. How are you?" Christine was more than a little surprised.

"I'm great. Just great. In fact—I'd like to celebrate. And I thought of you."

Christine frowned. Did the doctor have the right number? She hadn't even spoken to him in weeks.

"I'm listening," she managed.

"I just completed my residency and have been offered a position. Right here at General."

"That's wonderful. Congratulations."

"Thank you. So . . . I know this is . . . rather out of the blue. But I wondered if I could ask you to help me celebrate being a working, full-fledged doctor of medicine." He finished in rather a rush.

"I . . . I was just going out the door. Down to Hope Canteen."

"To help out?"

"Yes."

"Do they expect you?"

"Well . . . not definitely. I mean, I go when I can. We all do."

"So if you didn't show up, you wouldn't be breaking a promise."

Christine hesitated. "No . . . not really."

"Then would you mind changing your plans?"

Christine was caught totally off guard. "What . . . what did you have in mind?"

"Dinner."

"I've had dinner."

"Then would you come with me and watch me eat?" She could tell by his voice he was joking again. "Seriously," he hurried on, "I will grab a bite here at the cafeteria and pick you up about seven. There is a concert tonight at the Opera Hall—full orchestra. I thought we might catch that if you're interested. Then pop out for coffee afterward. Promise—I'll try to find something better than what you'd get here."

"A concert?"

"It's billed as a tribute to Mozart."

"Mozart?" She was sounding awfully dense, she knew.

"How about it?"

"I guess I could. Yes, that will be fine."

"Thanks. I'll pick you up at seven."

Christine cradled the phone, still in shock. The call was so totally unexpected. She had almost forgotten that Eric Carlton even existed. Without her daily trips to the hospital, she had pushed all thoughts of the whole experience from her mind. Now she stood dumbly looking down at her skirt and blouse, trying to get through her benumbed brain that if she was going to a concert instead of the service center, she had to change. But she wasn't moving.

"Who was it, dear? Your mother?"

Christine stirred. "No. No . . . a friend. I've been invited to a concert."

"That's nice. You need to get out more."

Christine turned and slowly climbed the steps to her room, her sweater still over her arm. She guessed she wouldn't be needing that either.

It had been so long since she had gone out for an evening of entertainment that she scarcely knew where to start in getting prepared. At last she shook out her mental cobwebs and headed for her closet. She had the lovely suit from Henry's wedding. She had scarcely worn it since. It had seemed a bit too dressy for church. She pulled it out and stood looking at it, then one hand reached out and brushed the smooth material. Yes, she would wear it. It should be fine for the concert.

She had showered that morning, but she decided it didn't seem right to put on the beautiful suit without first bathing. She sprinkled bath salts liberally in the water as she filled the tub. The pleasing aroma was deliciously jasmine. Not too strong, but rich enough to be noticed.

Once in her suit, she sat down at the dressing table. She would have to do something with her hair. Her usual casual style didn't go with the fancy suit at all. She wound it this way, tucked it up that way, and liked nothing she tried. At last she picked out some decorative combs Henry had given her one Christmas. She brushed it back and up, pinned it with the combs, then let it fall in a cascade about her shoulders. It wasn't perfect, to her thinking, but it would do.

She was just patting a bit of powder on her nose when she heard the doorbell. Gathering her purse and her self-confidence, she slowly descended the stairs.

She hardly recognized him as the same man without his stark hospital whites. A dapper, black-striped, double-breasted suit included a handkerchief that matched his checked tie tucked in the pocket. The white shirt fairly rustled with crispness. For one brief moment they stood and stared at each other. Then he seemed to recover and smiled. "Miss Delaney."

He held out a bouquet of flowers.

Christine noticed that Aunt Mary, who had answered the door, had not moved. First looking from one to the other, she then reached out a hand and took the flowers from Christine. "I'll take care for those for you if you like. You mustn't be late."

Christine managed a nod.

"Shall we?" He offered his arm, and Christine accepted it tentatively.

"It was nice to meet you, Mrs. Thatcher," he said with a nod of his head to Mary.

"Have a nice evening," she answered, and the door closed behind them.

He didn't say that she looked lovely. At least not verbally. But Christine got the clear message from his frank approval. He did thank her for accepting his last-minute invitation.

"It wasn't fair of me," he admitted as he helped her into the car. "But I just had to try. I thought of you, Christine, the moment I realized I had something to celebrate."

Christine was surprised. She had hardly remembered their encounters at the hospital.

"In fact, were I to be totally truthful, I'd have to admit that I've been doing a good deal of thinking about you over the recent months. But I wanted to get this residency thing out of the way," he said as he put the car in gear.

Christine flushed, not quite sure what she was to read into his words.

"I haven't even made it down to Hope Canteen like I'd planned."

Christine had noticed that—at first. Then it had slipped from her mind, and she'd forgotten all about it. She knew doctors were kept busy.

The concert turned out to be delightful. Christine felt herself becoming totally absorbed by the music. It had been so long since she had been able to sit and thoroughly enjoy something beyond her work and her family. And to be able to forget, momentarily, all the struggles and conflicts of the world. She felt herself relaxing, her mind clearing, her emotions soaring with the music.

Eric caught her eye and gave her a smile. For one moment she wondered if he might reach for her hand and spoil everything, but he did not and she was able to relax again. Soon she forgot everything but the music. The wonderful music that washed over and around her. When they played the slow movement of Mozart's piano concerto number 21 in C, she closed her eyes and rested against the seat back. *That is musical perfection,* she mused. Truly Mozart had been a genius. A gift to the world from the Creator of all things beautiful.

All too soon the concert ended, and Christine returned to reality. As they stood with the rest of the audience to offer one final applause to the orchestra, Christine felt both elated and let down. It had been such a wonderfully renewing and stimulating evening that she had hated for it to finish.

"Thank you," she whispered to her escort. "I can't tell you how much I enjoyed it."

He did take her hand then. Just long enough to give it a light squeeze. Then he released it again.

"It was," he agreed, "and doubly so for me, just watching your face."

She found herself flushing and was glad for the diversion of making their way through the exiting crowd.

He didn't ask where she'd like to go. She could tell he already had a restaurant in mind. It was softly lit with rich, plush seats and deep carpeting on the floors. She thought it must be terribly expensive and was about to protest when she remembered that this was his night of celebration. She would not spoil it for him.

They ordered coffee and dessert, the chocolate mousse. The coffee was rich yet mellow. Christine immediately deemed it the best coffee she'd ever tasted. He laughed. "Are you just comparing it to the hospital fare?" But she shook her head.

They visited easily in the elegant surroundings. He spoke of his work and inquired of Henry and Amber. He also asked about her work and how things were going at Hope Canteen.

"Your aunt seems to be a delightful person," he continued, and Christine launched into a description of her extended family.

Eventually he told her that he was the youngest of four children, born and raised in Calgary. His oldest brother was a university professor, his other brother an attorney, and his sister was married to a minister. She, with her husband and three children, had moved to Victoria. Those being the only grandchildren, the grandparents were missing the little ones.

From snippets of the conversation, Christine came to understand that his was one of the "old" families in the town.

This was confirmed to her when he told her where his folks lived and that his father had been in real estate and development, taking over the business from his father before him.

"Some of the buildings on Main Street were my grandfather's doing," he said simply without obvious boast.

He really is very pleasant, thought Christine as she listened to his account of family life. *And good-looking.* His eyes were especially nice. Very blue, framed by dark lashes. His hands were long and slim, like the hands of a pianist—or a surgeon. Christine was surprised she hadn't noticed these things before.

"I'd love to have you meet my folks," he continued, and Christine felt her stomach lurch.

Meet his folks. She was pretty sure she was not accustomed to their kind of living. She had been raised in the North in rather primitive surroundings, the daughter of a police officer. She was used to things being rugged and rustic. She was used to making do and going without. What could she possibly have in common with people who had helped build a city? The very thought frightened her. She tried to force a smile and murmured something like, perhaps one day, or some such noncommittal words, but she did hope that the day would not be soon.

True, she now had a job in a sophisticated city office and managed just fine. True, she presently lived with her Uncle Jonathan and Aunt Mary who had one of the nicest homes in Mount Royal. But it wasn't her home. She would go back to the North at the least opportunity. She wouldn't even need encouragement. And she was still hoping with all her heart that such opportunity would eventually come.

"It's been a lovely evening, but I really should be getting home."

He did not argue. "I still can't believe I'll actually be working days now—except when I am on call," he commented as he led her to the car door held open by the valet. "It's going to seem like I've been given my life back," he quipped.

Christine slid into the passenger side, and the valet closed her door. He moved around to Eric's side and, with a slight bow, held the door for him. Christine saw money change hands and the valet back away with a cheery, "Thank you. Good night to you, Dr. Carlton," as he tucked the bills in his pocket. *So he is known at this fancy restaurant,* Christine thought.

It was rather a quiet ride home. *Perhaps he is all talked out. Perhaps he is weary after a long day,* Christine surmised. In truth, she was glad for the chance to gather her thoughts.

"It's a shame this was the last concert of the season," he said, half turning toward her. She wondered where his thoughts had been. "They don't start again until September."

Christine had seen the announcement in the program.

"Well, we sure can't wait for that. What would you like to do?" he asked.

"I'm ... I'm not sure what you mean," Christine managed to answer.

"Am I being presumptuous? I was hoping you had enjoyed the evening."

"Oh, I did," she said quickly. *Maybe too quickly.*

"Just the music?" There was teasing in his voice again. She wasn't sure whether to tease back or be serious.

"No ... not just the music," she admitted shyly. "Every part of the evening."

"Then you will agree to go out again?"

She cast a glance his way. He wasn't teasing now.

"That depends. If ... if I ... if we both think it wise and ... and desirable, then—"

"I think it would be wise ... *and* desirable."

They were already pulling up in front of the house. The porch light was still on and a dim light shone out from the hall window, though Christine saw no light in the living room. *They must have already retired.*

"Then ... perhaps you'd like to call me," she said softly, "and we'll talk about it."

"I'll do that." He grinned and opened his door.

When he came around to Christine's side, he opened her door and waited for her to step out. "You're not leaving me your purse or a hankie or something so I have an excuse to call tomorrow?" he joked.

She shook her head. His easy banter made her wonder just what she should take seriously. *Perhaps a doctor needs a sense of humor—just to make it through some of his days,* she decided.

He tucked her arm in his and led her up the sidewalk. "I understand this is where your aunt fell."

"That's right."

"Well, we wouldn't want that to happen to you, would we, so I'll just have to hold on tight."

"My aunt fell on ice," she rejoined, but even as she said

the words she heard him chuckle.

Christine drew out her key, but she had no need of it. The door had been left unlocked.

He stepped back. The overhead porch fixture splashed down light on his head, making it look as if he was wearing an unusual halo. His face was shadowed, but she could hear the earnestness in his voice, even if she could not read his eyes. "I don't know when I've had such a pleasant evening, Christine. I felt like the luckiest guy in the hall tonight, and I'd like to do it again—real soon."

"There are no more concerts—remember?"

"We don't need a concert. We'll make our own music. At least we can go out to dinner—or picnic, or for a walk. Something. Anything."

She nodded. He must have seen the nod in the semi-darkness, for he whispered, "Good. I'll call you." Christine watched him walk away with a light step before she gently closed the door.

It was quiet in the house. She flicked off the porch light and proceeded up the stairs to her room. Her head was whirling. What was happening? In some ways he seemed so serious. In others so . . . so casual. She wasn't sure just how to interpret his manner, his intentions. She had a lot of thinking, a lot of praying to do before she could know her own mind.

She turned on the light to her room and began preparations for bed, but her mind was still totally preoccupied. She had to carefully think some things through before her emotions came into play. She had made a bad mistake before in a relationship. She did not wish to go down that kind of path again.

He does have faith in God. That was the place to start in her inventory. She would never allow herself to be involved with a nonbeliever again. But what else did she really know about him? *Henry liked him.* That was another big plus. She trusted her big brother's judgment of people.

He seems to have love and respect for his family. That was good. Family was very important to Christine.

He has a sense of humor. She supposed that was good, though she sometimes found it difficult to know if he was serious or teasing.

He's from a well-established, probably wealthy, family. That was not a plus in Christine's thinking. That part scared her. She could picture a mother, prim and sedate, lips tightly pursed, daring some slip of a girl to try to take her son away from her. She could imagine a stern, money-driven father, hands folded over an ample chest, peering out with cold eyes at another young gold digger out to get her hands on a share of the family wealth. It was not a pretty picture. Christine shook her head. She wanted no part of it.

Hastily she pulled her nightgown over her head and knelt to say her evening prayers. But she found it hard to concentrate. She liked Eric Carlton, she really did, but she was afraid of his family's wealth and prestige. How could she ever live up to the expectations that his family likely would have for her?

She said "Amen" but wondered if she had really talked to God with her rambling, troubling thoughts, or had she simply repeated by rote things she had been saying for many nights?

She turned out the light and climbed into her bed, her thoughts still in turmoil. *I don't know why I said he could call,* she chided herself. *This little charade can go nowhere. I must find the courage to tell him so when he phones.*

And with her mind firmly made up, Christine pulled the covers up to her chin and tried to quiet her troubled heart so she could sleep.

CHAPTER EIGHTEEN

Uncle Jonathan summoned Christine to the phone. When she lifted the receiver to her ear and said hello, the first word she heard was, "Dinner?"

"Eric?"

"Actually, this is Bob."

She recognized his voice. Had she thought more quickly—and dared—she could have responded, "Bob, I've been waiting for you to call. I'd love to." Just to give him a bit of his own medicine. But Christine was not one for that kind of joking. She merely flushed and felt confused.

"It's Eric," he said in a more serious tone when she had no reply. "How about dinner?"

"Tonight?"

"Tonight—if possible. If not—at your earliest opportunity."

"Not tonight. I have plans."

"Tomorrow?"

She was tempted to tell him that tomorrow would not work either. In fact, she expected to be busy for the rest of her life. But she knew she had to explain to him in person that there was no hope for a relationship. She dreaded the thought. She'd rather just run away and never need to face him again. But that would be the coward's way out.

"I . . . yes . . . I guess so. Tomorrow will work."

He must have known from her voice that she was hesitant, but he did not make comment.

"May I pick you up at six?"

"Six will be fine."

"Would you like fine dining—or something more relaxed and contemporary?"

"I . . . I really don't know . . . about the contemporary, I mean. What did you have in mind?"

"There's a new café on the south side where the younger crowd goes. It is quite casual."

"That sounds fine." She really didn't wish to wear the same suit two dates in a row.

"Great. See you at six."

Christine was troubled as she hung up the receiver. Was that really the way one was supposed to feel when accepting a date? She picked up her sweater and called to her aunt and uncle, "I won't be late," and left the house. The streetcar ride was not nearly long enough to quiet her jangled nerves. She entered Hope Canteen still feeling jittery. Jane, one of the other volunteers, was there to meet her. She seemed excited and grabbed Christine by both shoulders. "They've done it. They've done it," she said.

Christine could not imagine what had been done.

Just then Paula raced up with a broad, happy smile. "Finally," she said. "Finally it has happened. We'll get some real direction here."

Christine stepped back, disengaging Jane's hands. "What are you two talking about?"

"They have hired a chaplain—finally," Paula enthused.

It *was* good news. All the volunteers had been praying for a full-time chaplain to run the program. They felt that to really do an effective job of ministry, they needed leadership.

"Is it one of the pastors who has been volunteering?" asked Christine.

"No. No, this is someone entirely new."

"When does he start?"

"He's here—now. He's already got a little office. He's been talking to the volunteers. He says he wants to discuss things with each of us—just to get the feel of the place. You know. What's been done. What we hope to see accomplished. How we view the ministry. All that."

At last Christine smiled. It really was wonderful news. That was what they had been hoping for—praying for. A solid ministry—not just a coffee service.

"He's talking with Tommy right now."

Oh no. Not poor Tommy. Did Tommy even know what was going on? Surely this new chaplain would understand that Tommy really was an asset to the ministry. It was true he took occasional teasing from some of the young fellows, but once they got to know him, they seemed to accept him for who he was in spite of his handicaps.

"He wants to see you next."

Suddenly Christine felt nervous butterflies winging to and fro in her stomach. She couldn't have said why, but she felt even more uncertain than she had when she had gone for her job interview. She was to be next. What if this new chaplain decided she wasn't a good fit for this work? What if he took them on a path they were not willing to follow? What if he was expecting to run a coffeehouse instead of a ministry of hope? Could she continue to offer her services where all that was handed out was comfort foods and idle chatter?

For the first time Christine realized just how at home she had become in this ministry. She still grieved that the world was at war, but it had been some time since she had

struggled with whether she was one who should go overseas. Without her even realizing that it had happened, God
had put her mind at peace. For the moment, she was right
where she should be. She was serving just as she should
serve. This was a wondrous revelation, one that brought a
surge of joy to her heart. She should, all along, have trusted
Him to lead her. She had prayed for His direction, hadn't
she? Then why should she be surprised that He had led?
*"Not all of God's leading comes with detailed instructions or great
fanfare,"* she remembered hearing a pastor once say. *"Sometimes it is that still small voice. And perhaps—just perhaps, we are
not even aware of the voice. Just the sense of peace."*

And that was exactly what had happened to Christine.
That beautiful sense of God's peace. God's presence. God's
acceptance of where she was at in her life and what she was
doing. *"The absence of an inner conflict is one of life's richest
blessings,"* the pastor also had said. *"And it comes only from
the hand of God."*

That was it. She *could* trust Him. She could. As long as
she honestly sought to walk in His paths—she could trust
Him.

So why am I fretting now about this new chaplain? she asked
herself. *Isn't God in charge here too?*

Christine took a deep breath and moved forward to
take up her evening responsibilities and maybe even bring
some encouragement, new faith, to someone in the
crowded room. As usual, she breathed a prayer, "Lord, lead
me tonight to someone who has a heart open to you. When
I make that connection, give me the right words to speak.
May I speak with wisdom and love. In Jesus' name. Amen."

She had just carried a tray of coffee to a group of noisy
young men when Jane ran up to her. "It's your turn. He
wants to see you now. He's in the room we used to use for
storage."

Christine ignored those butterflies trying to get their

wings in motion and walked toward the former storage room. It wouldn't make much of an office.

The door was closed. She rapped and heard a man's voice bid her enter. He had a journal of some sort spread out before him, and he was busily writing in it. At the sound of her step, he lifted his head, then lowered it again to check his notes. "Miss Delaney, I believe."

She nodded. He was awfully young. Much too young to give proper leadership to such an important ministry. They had hoped for someone experienced. Someone solid. Older.

She swallowed and nodded her head again.

He smiled, stood, and extended his hand. "I'm Tim— Timothy Marcus," he said.

She was surprised at his firm handshake and open manner. She could feel calluses in the palm of his hand. *Straight off the farm* was her unexpected thought. She wasn't ready to say if that was good or bad. Would he be able to build rapport with all these young people? Then she remembered that many of them were straight off the farm too.

"Won't you take a seat," he invited, and Christine sat down.

She hardly recognized the former storage room. It had a fresh coat of light paint, making it look larger, more inviting. She could see that the desk was well used, but it too was freshly painted. A small chest with four drawers served as a filing cabinet, and the three chairs in the room were unmatched but looked serviceable. He even had a picture on the wall, of Jesus walking on the water. The caption read, "He can calm any storm if you'll let Him in your boat."

Christine clasped her hands tightly in her lap.

"I just had the most delightful conversation," he said, a smile playing about his mouth. "Thomas. Tommy, he prefers. You've worked with him."

Christine nodded.

"Such a wonderful young man. So open—so honest with God. So eager to share his faith. He was a . . . an . . . actually, I felt like God sent him to me to verify that this is where I am meant to be."

Christine could only stare.

"He has such . . . such simple . . . passion. I pray that God might make me more like him."

More like Tommy? Some segments of society labeled Tommy a retard. Crazy. A dolt or a fool. To be more like him seemed an unusual prayer. Christine now watched the young chaplain with new interest.

He turned back to the pages before him. "You've been here some time now."

Christine nodded. He leaned back in his chair, toying with the pencil he held in his broad hands. "Consistency is good for any ministry," he noted.

It was much more like a warm, informal visit than an interview. Christine was surprised at how quickly she was able to relax and share her heart. This young man really was there to serve, and he intended to do so with his whole being. With all the resources available. Young men and women were going off to war. They needed the assurance that God was with them. That they had made peace with their Maker through the sacrifice of His Son, the Savior. It was a matter of spiritual life and death.

Christine could not believe how long they talked. They shared many of the same thoughts and feelings. The same dreams and goals. The same sense of commitment. By the time she left the little office, she felt that surely God was going to raise the ministry of Hope Canteen to a new level.

"So what do you think of him?" Jane was quick to ask when Christine took her place back in the kitchenette.

Christine felt flushed with inner joy. "I think he'll do fine. His heart certainly—"

"A dreamboat like that and you're thinking of his

heart?" Paula cut in with a giggle.

Christine turned and stared. What in the world was Paula talking about? She hadn't even noticed if he was good-looking. What difference did that make? The important thing was whether or not he would throw himself into the work of Hope Canteen as an important ministry. His looks had little—nothing, actually—to do with it. She picked up the soda glasses she had just filled and took them out to the tables.

———

Christine was not looking forward to her next date with Eric. There was no way they had anything in common. There was no hope for any future relationship to develop— so why was she even going through the motions? It was ridiculous.

But she had made a commitment to herself to let him know this in person. She would see it through.

He arrived right on time at six. He was dressed in slacks and a casual shirt opened at the neck and sleeves rolled up to just below his elbows. He looked even more handsome than he had in his expensive-looking suit.

"Bob—at your service," he kidded when she opened the door. Then he openly appraised her full skirt and pink sweater and nodded. "You look great."

She did mumble a courtesy thank-you.

"I hope you like this place," he said as the car moved away from the curb. "It's a bit noisy at times. A lot of young servicemen go there. So, as you might well imagine, there's quite a collection of the young ladies from town as well."

Christine raised an eyebrow. She did hope this was not one of those offensive downtown pubs catering to all kinds of raucous and offensive behavior.

"They have good food—and after we've eaten, if we find

it's too noisy for decent conversation, we can go somewhere else."

How long a date is this to be? wondered Christine. *You told me dinner.* But she said nothing. She would work her way through the evening, and if she felt uncomfortable she would ask to be taken home.

The place was already filled with a young crowd. It was noisy; there was no arguing that. In fact, the entire feel was one of high energy. But it all looked like wholesome high spirits, and Christine did not feel at all uncomfortable, but rather invigorated. Eric found a table off in the corner where they could converse comfortably in spite of the hearty laughter and swirl of activity around them.

The food was indeed delicious. Christine soon found herself enjoying the evening in spite of her misgivings.

After they had eaten, Eric suggested they go for a drive along the river. They just drove and talked, enjoying the scenery and the warm breeze through the open car windows. He made no effort to park someplace along their route, and Christine appreciated the fact. It wasn't late when they arrived back at the house.

"I'm going to be on call for a series of nights now," he explained as they pulled up in front. "But I do want to see you again—soon. How about Sunday?"

Christine had failed to give her prepared speech. Now she chastised herself at the same time she found herself nodding in agreement.

"It will have to be rather early," he told her. "Morning service and a quick lunch. I need to be on the ward by two."

Christine nodded again.

"Tell you what. I'll take you to your church this time. But you must agree to come with me to mine next time. I want to show you off."

That didn't seem like the best reason to attend church, but Christine again nodded.

"If it's a Sunday when I have the day off, I'll have Mother invite you for dinner," he went on, and now Christine felt her stomach tighten. What could she say? She had already agreed, in a way.

He walked her to the door with further details about picking her up for church Sunday morning. When Christine entered the front hall, she bypassed the living room where she could hear voices. When there was a brief lull she called out, "I'm home," then went immediately up to her room.

Why did she feel so agitated? They'd had a delightful evening. He had been an enjoyable and thoughtful companion. She had seen admiring and envious glances of other young women. But the fact that he came from a well-to-do family hadn't made him a snob. Just because her uncle Jon and aunt Mary had money didn't mean they felt superior to others. She had been passing unfair judgment on his parents without even having met them. It wasn't right.

So why was she so uncomfortable? Was it because of Boyd? Had she been so hurt by her mistake of the past that she was afraid to commit herself again? But that wasn't right either. Nor was it fair to Eric. She must be able to accept him for who he was.

Christine prepared for bed, still wrestling with her conflicting emotions. *Okay*, she finally told herself. *I am wrong to prejudge—that I know. I am also wrong to refuse to give this new relationship a chance. I would be equally wrong to throw myself into something without careful thought and prayer. I need to take this . . . this friendship one cautious step at a time, allowing God to lead me. Just as He has given me peace about working at Hope Canteen, so I believe He can give me peace over this part of my life.*

She felt much better as she picked up her Bible for her evening reading. It fell open to Proverbs as she spread it in her hands, and words she had underlined and promised to live by drew her attention. "Trust in the Lord with all thine heart; and lean not unto thine own understanding. In all thy ways acknowledge him, and he shall direct thy paths."

Yes, Lord, she whispered. *I will trust you with this. I have no idea what and how you might bring the right thing to pass, but it will be rather exciting to walk with you to find out.*

She felt much quieter and more confident as she later knelt in prayer.

Sunday, she thought as she began undressing for bed. Sunday Eric was to visit her church. He would probably talk with her aunt and uncle. Perhaps Aunt Mary would even invite him for dinner—if there was time. She trusted their judgment. How they responded to Eric would surely give her some kind of direction as to how she should proceed. That thought put Christine's mind further at ease. She was not in this totally alone. She had other heads and hearts to guide her.

And she would meet his folks, if that was what he wanted. She would try to have an open mind. Perhaps they were decent, God-fearing people with as much desire to follow the Lord's leading as she herself. They, too, could act as guide to the relationship Eric seemingly wished to establish. She would seek to be sensitive to them as well.

Oh, I wish Mom and Dad were here, she found herself thinking as she climbed into bed. Choosing a life's partner was a serious matter, and though she knew that ultimately she would be the one who needed to make the final choice, she still felt thankful that she would not need to rely on her own conclusions. God had placed many people in her life who could act as signposts as to what path she should take.

Feeling much more at ease, Christine prepared for sleep, which she did hope would come quickly. Tomorrow would be another busy day, and she fully intended to once again spend the evening at Hope Canteen. A young woman she had spoken to on her last night there seemed very open to the good news of the gospel. Christine's last thoughts were whispered prayers that the girl might return with a readiness to make a commitment. "God, you know all about Krista. Bring her back to us. Bring her to you."

CHAPTER NINETEEN

Hope Canteen had closed its doors for the night, and the volunteers were chatting as they did their clean-up duties. There was a good deal of excitement as they compared notes. Krista had returned and had prayed with Christine to receive Christ as her Savior. A young man also prayed in a similar fashion, and another young man had promised to do some serious thinking while two others had said they would be back to talk further. It was the most promising response they'd had on any one night.

Smiling, Timothy Marcus approached the working group, an opened bottle of orange soda in his hand. "Good job, team. That young airman really meant business. Would you believe this was his first contact with the Gospel of Christ? And the fellow from the navy. He'd been raised in church—was rather a modern-day Jonah—but he knew he'd never run from God."

He reached out and laid a hand on Tommy's shoulder. "Do you know what he told me? He said you were the first one to put his mind at ease about coming here. Your smile and your 'Come on in, sailor.' He'd been about ready to turn around and run."

He patted Tommy's back appreciatively. Tommy beamed around on the group, then turned back to Pastor Tim with tears in his eyes.

"Thank you, everyone, for your dedication to Christ. Not to a program nor a cause—but to Christ. Remember, none of us works for Hope Canteen—we work for Him," the young chaplain finished, pointing heavenward.

Christine was sure it was an important reminder.

He set aside his pop and picked up a pail and dishcloth. "Where are you on the tables?" he asked Paula as he moved out to give a hand. With everyone pitching in, it did not take long for the remainder of the work to be done. Soon they were gathering jackets and sweaters and heading for the various streetcar stops, calling their good-nights to one another.

"Do you go my way?"

Christine was surprised to hear the voice right beside her. It was Pastor Tim.

"I catch the streetcar at the corner," she answered.

"Going north or south?"

"South."

"So do I."

She had not yet heard which part of the city he called home.

"How far do you go?" he asked.

"Almost as far as the streetcar goes," she said with a laugh.

"So do I. Just short of Mount Royal. I'm staying with my grandparents until I find a spot of my own."

"Oh. I'm staying with my aunt and uncle."

"It's great having family in the city."

Christine silently agreed.

He chuckled. "Of course the city wasn't my first choice.

I would have much rather been sent to some little rural church or even a smaller town." He shrugged his shoulders. "But here I am."

"It wouldn't be my first choice either," admitted Christine.

"That rather surprises me. You seem like a city girl."

"Me? Afraid not."

"You from the farm?"

"I'm from the North."

"The North?" He sounded surprised.

"My dad is a Mountie. I grew up in the North."

"And you loved it."

"I loved it."

"You don't really need to say it. Your voice says it for you. So what did you like about the North?"

And as they waited for their streetcar to arrive, Christine told him. The more she talked, the more nostalgic she felt. She knew she'd best stop before she found herself in tears. "Where did you grow up?" she asked in order to divert herself.

"Camrose."

"I've never been to Camrose."

"You should come. It's a great place. Farming community."

"Your father was a farmer?"

"No. He had a dry-goods store. But I worked on a farm from the time I was big enough to lift a fork. For my uncle. He has a farm just on the edge of town. I used to ride my bike over from school as soon as I was done for the day. Nearly pestered him to death with, *What could I do?* He finally decided as long as I was taggin' along behind him anyway, he might as well put me to work. So he hired me. I love the farm."

"But you're a preacher instead."

"Yeah." His tone sounded nostalgic too. "Guess it was

rather like Amos, the shepherd prophet, or like Elisha. I believe God, figuratively speaking, was telling me to break up my plow, offer up the oxen as sacrifices, and go preach. What could I do?"

Christine saw the teasing grin but also the seriousness in the dark eyes. Indeed, what could he do?

Their streetcar pulled up and they climbed aboard. They took a seat together and continued to talk.

"I've been thinking of starting a Sunday morning worship service," Tim went on. "I know there are many of these young servicemen who wouldn't feel comfortable going to one of the city churches, but who might attend a service at the canteen. What do you think?"

Christine thought a moment. "I think it's a good idea."

"We'd need a little nucleus of volunteers."

She nodded.

"It might start out really small—but I hope the numbers would build."

"It would help if we had a piano—or something."

"I play the guitar, and I have a friend who plays the accordion. It would work for a while. I don't know where we would get a piano. Do you play?"

Christine shook her head. She had always felt sorry she hadn't been able to learn to play. Her mother played so beautifully, but there had been no instrument in the North on which to learn.

"Do you know if any of the other girls do?"

"I heard something about Bernice playing."

"Bernice? I don't remember her."

"No, she hasn't been around much lately. Last I heard, she had become interested in one of the young airmen. There was even talk of an engagement, but I think he was shipped out. I've not seen her or heard of her for several weeks."

She saw his concerned look. There was the risk of

wrong relationships being established when young men and women were put into such intimate contact in wartime.

"Is her name on our list? I'd like to get in touch with her and see how she is doing."

"I'm not sure. But Violet might know how to find her. They seemed quite close."

"I do not like to ask our volunteers to give up their own churches, but if we started a Sunday service, would you be available to help?"

"I would hate to miss my own service," Christine said honestly. "But I'll pray about it."

"That's all I would ask."

The streetcar swayed around a corner and rumbled along the street leading out to Mount Royal. Christine knew he would soon be disembarking. She'd been told he not only spent long hours at his office, he also walked the streets during the day, visiting some of the cafés and bars, handing out information about the canteen, and issuing invitations. She was sure he was feeling weary by now.

"Well, this is my stop coming up," he announced as he stood to his feet. "Thanks again for your help. We would never be able to run the canteen without the services of the volunteers."

Christine smiled just before he turned and lightly sprang down the steps. She heard his retreating whistle before the streetcar moved on. The song was "Count Your Blessings." She smiled again.

———

As always, it was difficult to find an empty seat as Eric and Christine were ushered into church on Sunday. "I see why you say you need to build," he whispered in her ear.

She saw a few heads turn as they made their way almost

to the front of the sanctuary—mostly young people who no doubt were wondering if they were "an item." Well, she wasn't there to worry about that. She was there to worship.

They squeezed in beside an older couple whom Christine did not know, smiled a good-morning, and picked up the hymnal to share.

She was surprised at his wonderful tenor voice, and he sang out heartily. It seemed to inspire those around them—including herself. She paid more attention to the hymns and sang more fervently than usual.

She stole a glance his way a few times during the service and noticed that the minister had his full attention. Once she even heard a whispered "Amen." She liked that. She liked to think he had come to church to worship God—not to spend time with a girl, even if the girl was she.

He had been invited to dinner, so he drove her straight to the house. Aunt Mary had assured him that they appreciated his time schedule, and dinner would be served as quickly as possible. She planned the meal accordingly, having a casserole in the oven and the salad already made and in the refrigerator. Lucy had volunteered to stay home to prepare the meal, but Mary would have none of it.

"No need for you to miss church," Christine had heard her say. "We'll just fix a simple meal that we can serve promptly." So that was what they did.

By the time Christine and Eric arrived, the warm, inviting smell of the hot biscuits met them as they stepped through the door into the hall.

"Umm," said Eric. "I think I'm going to like this restaurant," as Aunt Mary appeared, biscuit pan in hand, to welcome them and tell them everything was ready.

The meal was very pleasant. Eric, quite familiar with Jon's business in the city, visited easily with Jon and Mary. Jon, in turn, knew of Eric's family, though they were not actually acquainted. Only occasionally did Eric add his trademark humor to the conversation. Christine was thankful that he seemed to know where to draw the line. It was as important to know when not to engage in banter as to know when to put it to use, in her thinking.

She was aware that even though Eric seemed relaxed and enjoyed conversing with the others at the table, he was also keeping a careful eye on the clock. Apparently he took his responsibilities seriously as well. That earned another plus chalk mark on her growing list of personal assets.

They enjoyed lemon pie and a second cup of coffee, then with a glance clockward, Eric placed his napkin on the table. "This has been most delightful," he said, sending a warm smile Mary's way, "but I see my time has quickly gone. I'm afraid I must excuse myself. Thank you so much for a delicious dinner."

He turned to Lucy, who always joined them at the table on Sunday. "You are a wonderful cook, Mrs. Taylor. I'm surprised that word hasn't gotten out to the Palliser Hotel. I'm sure they'd love to steal you away for their dining room kitchen, if they knew."

Lucy waved aside the compliment, but her cheeks flushed with pleasure.

"You needn't see me out," Eric said, laying a hand on Christine's shoulder. "Enjoy your coffee. I'll call you later."

With another acknowledgment of his host and hostess, he left the dining room.

"What a pleasant young man," said Aunt Mary.

"Yes," said Uncle Jonathan. "You've chosen well, Christine. Your folks would be pleased."

Christine felt her cheeks burn. She had not yet "chosen." She still wasn't sure how she would choose should she be given the opportunity. But was it wise to protest the assumption seemingly made? She wasn't sure of that either. They had been dating. She let the statement pass.

Christine had a new round of nerves the Sunday they were to visit Eric's church. It was a beautiful building but not ostentatious, and the worshipers seemed as warm and enthusiastic as in her own church. She felt comfortable from the moment she sat in the oak pew and joined in the singing of familiar hymns.

The minister presented a thought-provoking message, and Christine heard many amens to the inspiring challenge. So enrapt was she with all that was taking place she almost forgot that they were to go to Eric's home for dinner.

But when the last song had been sung, the last amen pronounced, Eric managed to find her gloved hand. He gave it the slightest squeeze. "Come," he whispered, "I'll introduce you to my folks."

"Can't we wait until we get to your house?" she asked nervously, hoping for some time to get herself together.

"My brothers and their wives want to meet you too. They won't be coming for dinner. Had other plans." He looked into her face a moment and said, "You don't have a thing to worry about, Christine—they'll think you're great, just like I do."

Christine gave a small smile in return for his and allowed herself to be led out to the foyer. It was already crowded with people busily engaged in conversation. Eric headed straight for a group off to the left. Christine assumed he must have told them all where he'd meet them.

His two brothers were as fair as he. One was a shade taller and the other just a bit heftier, but she could have told in a minute that the three were brothers. The young women standing with them both looked very nice. Even with her inexperience in such matters, Christine could tell that their suits had come from the city's best shops. As Eric led her up to the group, they fell silent. Christine decided they were sizing up this new girl on Eric's arm. She wondered momentarily just how many other young women Eric had brought to meet the family in the past. Her eyes circled the group, and she saw they all returned her smile. That was a comfort.

A woman to one side with her back to them was deep in conversation with another woman of the church. Eric looked toward her and shook his head. "My mother," he whispered, but there was respect and love in his voice. "She's always having committee meetings—even in the foyer."

She must have heard him, for she swung around quickly. "Eric."

She had very kind eyes. And the easiest, most sincere smile Christine had ever seen. She turned the full warmth of it on Christine now.

"And this must be Christine," she said, reaching out with both hands.

Christine did hope the woman wasn't going to go overboard and embarrass her with a gushy embrace. But though she took Christine's hands in both of her own, she went no further. "I'm so pleased to meet you," she said, and she sounded most genuine. Christine liked her immediately.

Eric's father was a bit more effusive in his greeting. Though there was nothing in his manner that was offensive, Christine got the distinct impression that he thought it about time his youngest son settled down. He also seemed to assume Eric had already made his choice, and both through his words and manner indicated his hearty approval. Christine felt her cheeks growing warm. *Why do people jump to such quick conclusions?* she wondered.

She was then introduced to the other family members. Each one was courteous and gracious. She supposed she should have felt relief—but for some reason she could not define, she did not. It was as though they all had concluded that she and Eric were already an item. That she was "bound" before even making the decision. It made her uncomfortable. They had only shared a few dates. What had he been telling them?

The home was elaborate, as Christine had expected. The dinner was delicious, as she also would have expected. They were most cordial, very sincere in their faith, entirely dedicated to family as Christine could tell when Mrs. Carlton showed pictures of her daughter, son-in-law, and grandchildren out in Victoria. But Christine was not able to relax. *I don't belong here* kept playing through her mind, though she could not have said why.

What girl wouldn't feel uniquely blessed to be welcomed into such a family? And by such a nice-looking, well-mannered young doctor—one who shared her faith and seemed to care about her deeply? It didn't make any sense that she hesitated. No sense at all.

She tried to push the thoughts aside and enter into the dinner conversation.

"Christine grew up in the North," Eric announced.

"The North. How interesting." This, with a smile, from his mother.

"My father is with the RCMP," she offered.

"RCMP. We have them to thank that the West was settled in such a civilized fashion," said Mr. Carlton. "My father, who helped build this town, said they never had one bit of trouble with the local Indian tribes—thanks largely to the RCMP, the North West Mounted Police as it was known back then."

Christine nodded. She knew the history of the Force and had often begged for stories of its beginning as she'd been tucked in bed at night.

"The natives trusted them," Mr. Carlton noted. "Learned soon enough that they'd take no nonsense from renegade whites any more than they would from the Indians."

Again Christine nodded.

"Well—they've done a good job of it. Hats off to your father and his fellows."

Christine felt a moment of pride.

"Her brother is also an officer," Eric went on.

"Is he up north as well?"

"No. No—he's stationed down in the South."

"He was in a bad auto accident last Easter," Eric explained. "That's when I met Christine. She came often to the hospital."

"Well—it's an ill wind that blows no good, as they say," said his father. "I wouldn't wish an auto accident on anyone, but at least this one brought the two of you together." His jovial smile and words left Christine feeling uneasy. Another assumption. She shivered slightly.

Eric must have noticed. "Are you cool? Would you like me to close the window?"

"No. I'm fine. Thank you," she managed, but she was glad to wrap trembling fingers around her warm coffee cup.

———

"My folks loved you," Eric told her later as he drove her home.

From somewhere deep inside she found some courage.

"Eric, I . . . I liked your parents too. But don't you think—I mean everything seems to be moving too fast. Folks are assuming things that . . . that we have not even discussed. I feel rather . . . rather like I'm being pushed over a cliff or caught in the rapids. I—"

He laughed. "Well—your northern roots are sure showing there. Caught in the rapids? Not many rapids around here."

Christine flushed.

"You know what I was trying to say," she said seriously.

"They don't mean to be taking certain things for granted," he defended. "I guess I have raved about you a bit. And then when they met you and realized that I didn't exaggerate—that you are everything I said—of course they jumped to conclusions. After all, I have finished my training and I'm ready to settle down. Why wouldn't they think—"

"But they're wrong. We have never even discussed any—future plans. It—"

"Shall we discuss them now?"

To her amazement he pulled the car to the side of the street and stopped. Then turned to her, as serious as she had ever seen him. She flushed.

"Eric," she managed to blurt out before he could say any more. "We hardly know one another. I don't think that one can even think of anything so . . . so important without—"

But he hushed her. "I know there are many things we haven't learned about one another yet. I know that. But, Christine, everything I do know about you . . . fascinates me. No, let me finish. It's not like I haven't known any other girls. I have. And it's not that I haven't had opportunities to form other relationships."

She could well imagine that was the truth. With his good looks and suave ways, young women would be tripping over each other to get to him.

"But I haven't met any others like you," he continued. "I really haven't. You are not just attractive—and I admit that has its draw." The teasing showed in his eyes, but they quickly became serious again. "But it's more than that. Much more than that. I like your devotion. Your commitment to your family and your Lord. I like the way you smile, even the way you frown. I like your class—"

"Please, Eric," she begged. "Please."

He stopped.

One arm spanned the distance between them, resting on the back of the car seat. Fingers toyed with a lock of her hair that hung over her shoulder. It was the first he had touched her like that. It was unsettling.

"I . . . I like you too," she stammered. "I don't deny that. I keep telling myself just how fortunate I am that you . . . even noticed me. But I think . . . well . . . I think we are moving too fast. I haven't had time to think. Time to pray. A lifetime is a long time, Eric. I . . . I made a wrong choice once. I very nearly married a man who . . . who was not at all right for me. I don't want to make that kind of mistake again. Can you understand that? I need time. I have to be sure."

He wrapped the curl around his finger and nodded, but there was pain in his blue eyes. "I understand," he agreed. "If you need time to pray—"

"No, Eric. Not just me. I want you to pray too. To honestly seek God's will in this. We both have to be sure. It's not just what *we* want—it's what *He* wants for us."

He nodded. "I can't argue with that."

They were both silent. Christine was inwardly praying. She wasn't sure what Eric was thinking.

"So where do we go from here?" he asked. There was pleading in his tone, even though he did not express it in words.

Christine felt her shoulders slump. "I'm not sure."

After another time of silence, she spoke again. "How about if we agree to earnestly, honestly, pray about it for a week? Then call me."

" 'Earnestly, honestly,' " he repeated. Then he nodded. "Okay."

He continued to finger her hair, watching the way the

curl wrapped tightly about his finger. "You want to go home now?"

"Please."

He surprised her by leaning forward and gently placing a kiss on the lock of hair. Then he let it slip from his finger and turned to start the car.

CHAPTER TWENTY

Christine began the week by rising early and spending some extra time in Bible study and prayer. She did want God's will for her life. She really did. How could she know what His will was? "Ask and ye shall receive," Scripture said. Christine was intent on asking.

Where do I start looking for His answer? she questioned herself. Well, why not start at the beginning? She opened to the book of Genesis. Monday morning's scripture reading was the story of creation. *In the beginning God . . .* she read. And that was just where she must begin, she concluded. With God. With understanding who He was and is. With the recognition that He had a plan—that it was within His right to have a plan and direction that would bring good to her life.

She steadily read through the first days of creation. God saw it was good. He was pleased with what He had created. *Let us make man in our image . . .* the account went on. And God did. *It is not good that the man should be alone* caught Christine's eye. *I will make him an help meet for him.* She jotted that down under Number One on the notebook page before her. God planned for man and woman to be joined in partnership. She put a little checkmark beside it. She need not fear that it was wrong for her to marry.

But the result of the first partnership was less than desired. Eve, tempted by the serpent, also introduced Adam to sin.

Number Two, wrote Christine. To fulfill God's plan, both members of the partnership must seek to follow Him. She placed another checkmark. Eric, too, was seeking God's will.

She read on. God had come looking for Adam and Eve. He had even supplied clothing to cover them, indicating His love and forgiveness—for both of them, not just one or the other. But they had been driven from the garden.

Point Number Three. If and when we do make an error, God still loves us and can and will forgive if we are repentant. But there are still consequences.

She had made a mistake in the past in promising to yoke her life with a nonbeliever. She had been forgiven, for which she was truly thankful. The consequences had been a disturbed and broken heart and the subsequent struggle with relationships.

But now she felt strongly that it was time to move on. Surely she was not wrong to honestly seek the partner that God had in mind for her. But was that one specific man? Or was there a broader field from which she might choose as long as she stayed within God's guidelines? She wasn't sure.

So far, Eric Carlton's character and personality showed only positive traits. The only negative, she realized, was the fact there was little chance that Dr. Eric Carlton would ever be heading to the North. There were not even outpost clinics there, let alone hospitals. No, it did not seem that Eric Carlton fit at all with her dream of returning to the land and people she loved. Was that why her heart was so disturbed? Yes. Yes, she supposed it was.

Hadn't her mother once said, *"Sometimes the way God chooses to lead us is through our own disquieted spirit"*? Well, her spirit was disquieted. Did that mean God was trying to tell her that this relationship was not of His choosing? She didn't know. She really didn't know. What she did know was that she could not go ahead with it until her spirit was at rest.

Christine closed the Bible and knelt in prayer. To her usual daily requests, she added fervent supplication for guidance.

She still felt uneasy as she stood to her feet, but from somewhere deep within, a little voice was whispering, *Trust. Just trust Him. He'll show the way.* And Christine stilled her troubled heart and agreed to be patient.

———

Christine went through her day's usual routine. By all outward appearances nothing had changed. Inwardly, she felt her whole world had been turned upside down. Or was it just on hold while she struggled to find what her next step should be?

Henry called with the news they were all doing fine. Gradually the pieces to his memory puzzle seemed to be falling into place. That was very good news. Amber, though still grieving the loss of their unborn child, was now able to look ahead and dream that in the future another baby would fill her heart and life. Danny did not seem any the worse for the accident.

"Do you ever see that young doctor?" Henry asked nonchalantly. "What was his name—Dr. Carlson?"

"Dr. Carlton, yes," Christine admitted. "He has finished his residency, and I've been seeing him."

"I was impressed with him," Henry went on. "I liked the

way his professionalism didn't get in the way of genuine care for his patient."

Christine changed the topic of conversation. She spoke for several minutes about Hope Canteen, then asked Henry about his work.

Henry groaned. "Laray just got his transfer. Boy, am I going to miss him."

Christine was caught off guard. She hadn't even thought of him for some time.

"Where?" she managed to ask.

"Beaver River. Imagine that. That's where Mom and Dad started."

Christine felt a little shock go all through her body. Laray was going north. How ironic it seemed. Could it possibly have anything to do with her?

"Did he request it?" she found herself asking.

"No. No, it just came out of the blue. Funny thing, eh?"

"Yes," she mumbled. "Yes, I guess it is."

"He's never worked with dogs, and after what that bear did to him, I worry a bit. Hope a dog never threatens to attack him, or he might panic. Dogs can sense your fear. You have to handle them. . . ."

Henry went on, but Christine was not listening. She loved the dogs. Loved working a team. Loved the sound of the yips and yaps as they voiced their eagerness to run. Loved the squeal of the sled runners on the coldness of packed snow. The scrunch of the snowshoes. The miniature clouds of frozen breath that billowed out as one ran through the frost of a crisp morning. *Does Henry miss all that?* she wondered.

"I'd better let you go," Henry was saying. "Don't want you late at Hope."

Christine knew he wasn't very taken with the term "canteen," and he always called the small mission center by the single word. But finding a friendly, open-sounding name was important in attracting young men and women.

Her fingers were trembling as she hung up the phone. *Laray is going north. He said, 'Just drop a note.' Does this mean...?*

She shook her head and started for the door, purse in hand. *Don't be foolish,* she scolded herself. *Many Mounties are sent north. Just because Maurice Laray happens to be one of them has nothing to do with you. Don't go complicating things further.*

———————

Tensions ran high that night at Hope Canteen. The war in Europe had escalated, and news of the Allies was not good. A new wave of recruits was soon to be sent overseas. Though their excitement could be heard in their voices, Christine felt that, in their saner moments, fear filled those young hearts too. Several sought to find some kind of solid anchor before being shipped out.

Pastor Tim mingled with the crowd, passing from one table to another, greeting various ones as he went, slapping shoulders, shaking hands. Even getting involved in a game of darts. No bets—betting was not allowed on any game in the canteen. Christine watched as he flipped a chair and straddled it, leaning his arms on its back. Three young fellows in navy uniforms were leaning slightly forward, listening intently to whatever it was the pastor was saying. He was so casual about it. But she didn't know anyone who could cut to the heart of a matter more quickly than this young minister. He didn't just talk, though. He listened. He was listening now as one of the young men spoke. *He's very good,* she thought. *And very devoted.* She admired him.

He'd be good in the North, she found herself thinking. *He listens well. But he leads too. I wonder if he has ever considered a northern mission? Wouldn't it be a wonder if God led...?*

She stopped. What reason did she have to think Pastor

Tim might include her in any of his plans? Well, she had to honestly admit, he had shown some interest in her. Perhaps . . .

Christine checked herself. The direction her thoughts had unexpectedly taken brought a flush to her cheeks. *Now,* said an inner voice, *you are not only wanting to plan your own life; you are mapping out the plan for others too.* She felt humbled and chagrined.

She carefully guarded her thoughts throughout the remainder of the evening. Once again the group of volunteers shared experiences as they worked together on cleanup. Another young man had made a commitment to faith, and a second one had made an appointment to meet with Pastor Tim the next day. He hadn't been quite brave enough to speak his heart with his buddies sharing the table.

Once again the young pastor and Christine fell into step and walked to the streetcar stop together.

"Are you as weary as I am?" he asked her.

Christine did not admit that she had gotten little sleep the night before and had been up extra early so she could search the Scriptures. Yes, she was weary.

"But it's worth it," he went on. "Just think—the angels are celebrating tonight. Another lost sheep has entered the fold."

It was a wonderful thought. Christine smiled with him.

"I sometimes ask myself, 'What do I do when this nightmare is over? When the troops are all safely home again—for those who come home, that is. Where will God lead me then?' "

Don't you say it—or even think it, Christine scolded herself. *For you to even suggest the North would be wrong.* She bit her tongue.

"Well, I don't need to worry about that," Tim said comfortably. "He'll show me. But it is rather exciting to think about what could be next. I never would have thought of serving here—but it's been awfully rewarding. I can't quite imagine being any other place. I guess that's how it is—how it is supposed to be—when we are where God wants us. When we are *in step*, so to speak."

Christine nodded. In step with God. That was exactly where she wanted to be.

The streetcar came and they boarded, talking about the day, the future, the horrors of war. So Christine was totally unprepared when he asked, seemingly out of nowhere, "Are you seeing anyone?"

"Yes," she answered easily, surprising even herself. "Yes, I am."

He nodded. "I couldn't imagine you *not* being taken," he said with a wry smile.

But I'm not really taken, Christine wished to argue and was surprised by the feeling that, yes, she was. In a way, she *was* taken.

"Tell me about him," he invited.

"He's . . . he's a doctor I met when my brother and his wife were in hospital."

"A doctor?" He lifted an eyebrow.

"He's very nice," Christine found herself going on. "He grew up right here in Calgary."

"Do you—have you reached an understanding?"

For some reason she did not resent his interest. It seemed perfectly in order.

"I've not noticed a ring on your finger," he added, then said with a grin, "I did check, I admit."

Christine flushed.

Suddenly she saw the man beside her not just as a very attractive young man, not as a ticket to her beloved North, but as a man of God. She half turned to him.

"I've felt . . . confused. You see, I almost made a bad mistake. I was engaged to a nonbeliever for a time. When that was over, it left me . . . scared. Doubtful of my own ability to ... to know how to choose. I've asked—well, we've decided to take a week and each seek God's will for our lives. For any future relationship. I ... I really won't be able to answer your question until the week is up."

His eyes had become thoughtful as he listened. She lowered her gaze. There was silence.

"I admire you. Both of you," the young minister said. "If every couple sought God's direction, there would undoubtedly be stronger, more secure and happy homes. And fewer trips to divorce courts. Fewer children left blaming themselves over events beyond their control."

Christine nodded. Those were the words she would have expected a minister to say.

But his next words were not. "Christine, I will seek to honestly pray for God's will—not mine—to guide your life, knowing that His will might be in conflict with my own human desire."

Her eyes widened. Was he saying ... ? Yes, she feared he was.

She was glad his stop was approaching. "I'll be praying—but I admit I'll also be watching that finger," he whispered with a wry grin as he got up to leave.

———

All through the week Christine spent her early mornings in searching the Scriptures and prayer, writing down in her notebook any truths that seemed applicable to her present quandary. Her heart and mind seemed to be no closer to her solution than before. Laray was going north. Pastor Tim might even be led of God to work in an Indian mission. She could envision him there. Yet it was Eric who had asked for her commitment. Eric who somehow was constantly in her thoughts. Eric who had endeared himself to her. She saw again his toying with her hair, his leaning over to kiss the single tress. It was like a gently given promise. But Eric in the North? She could not imagine it.

Christine felt panic-stricken. The week was drawing to a close. Eric would be calling her to hear her answer. What was she to say? She prayed that whatever it was she concluded to her search, he would be in agreement. What if she decided that they should continue the relationship and he decided it was over? What would they do then? Obviously it would end, and she'd be left again with a broken heart. Was that to be one of the consequences of her prior disobedience? Christine hoped not. Prayed not.

But she steeled her heart for the worst, yet hoping for . . . what?

CHAPTER TWENTY-ONE

On Saturday, only one day from their agreed deadline, Christine was getting desperate for an answer. She didn't really feel any closer to knowing what God wanted for her.

I will stay in my room and read and pray until I hear from the Lord, she told herself. She breathed a short prayer, asking for God to give wisdom and understanding as she reached for her Bible.

She had worked her way through the book of Genesis, making notes as she went. But she did not feel that, other than general guidelines, Genesis had given her an answer to her particular dilemma. She moved on to the familiar stories of Exodus. The slavery of the people, the birth and miraculous protection of the infant Moses. His sin in killing the Egyptian that resulted in his flight to the desert. She had heard the stories in Sunday school, in family Bible reading, and had read them a number of times herself. She concluded that Moses' flight really had little to do with Eric's rightful place in her life.

She moved on to the account of the burning bush. Moses certainly had not been expecting to encounter the

Hebrew God in the middle of the desert—and in such a strange, unheard-of way.

"Take off your sandals," God said.

Christine stopped reading. *"Take off your sandals." What does that mean?*

Certainly it was a cultural thing. But what was the significance?

Christine began to ponder the words, something she had not done previously with this passage. Sandals were necessary for protection in the desert. Moses needed them. But God told him to take them off, to lay them aside. Nothing Moses possessed of earthly connection or material goods prepared him to stand in the very presence of God. He was before a holy God, standing on holy ground. He was to show a proper humility of spirit.

Yet the very fact that God was there, speaking to him, was an indication that this holy, all-powerful God was willing to stoop down and intervene on behalf of His people. But before He could do great things, it had to be understood just who He was. *"Do you know who I am?"* He might have been asking. Through this seemingly simple action, God was confronting Moses. *"Moses—I am God. I am your God."* And as Moses understood, he fell on his face.

After a few moments of contemplation, Christine read on about God giving Moses a task to perform. An awesome task. One Moses had not sought. Nor did he feel capable of carrying it through. *"You've made a mistake here, Lord,"* he seemed to be saying. *"I'm not your man. They'll never listen to me."*

Christine thought back to when she and Henry were children and loved to act out Bible stories. Henry had always made a very impressive Moses. He would strike his brow and stagger around, calling out, "Oh, not me. Not me. I can't do it. They won't listen to me. I'm on the lam. Don't send me back, God. They might kill me. And I can't even talk right."

He would continue in this manner until they fell in a heap in a fit of giggles. She smiled now just thinking of it.

She always got to play the part of God, telling Moses there would be no change of plans. Once she had even whacked Henry on the leg, telling him to get up and get on with the task. That had not gone over well with either Henry or her folks.

"God didn't hit him," Henry had stated firmly, rubbing the spot.

"He should have," Christine maintained. "He was acting like a baby."

She thought of that now. *"He was acting like a baby."* How often had she acted like a baby, she wondered, when God gave her directions?

"What is that in your hand?" she read next.

Did Moses wonder why God had to ask such a question? Surely He could see what Moses had in his hand. No, the question was not asked because God needed to know. Moses needed to know.

"A staff."

He might have said, "My staff." It represented most of Moses' life. He was a shepherd. The staff was needed to protect himself and the sheep from marauders, to guide the sheep, to instruct the sheep. It was Moses' tool of the trade. His money in the bank. His sense of security. When he was out alone in the desert, it was about all he had.

"Throw it on the ground."

How well she remembered this part of the story. She had always felt so powerful, so totally in control when she ordered Henry to throw down his staff, which was either one of her mother's kitchen spoons or a small stick from the firebox.

Henry reacted according to their own unwritten script.

He would clutch whatever it was he was holding, close his eyes, and sway back and forth. "I can't. I can't," he would moan and groan. "It's mine. I don't want to give it up. I want to keep it. Please. Please," and he would fall on his knees, begging.

She smiled, then quickly sobered. It wasn't funny anymore. Suddenly she saw a totally different picture. The staff was no longer a piece of wood. It was whatever one was clinging to that kept one from accepting God's plan.

"Throw it on the ground," God said. *"Give it up."*

Tears began to squeeze from under Christine's eyelids and roll down her cheeks. Was there something in her life that kept God from being free to lead her? Was it the sense of unforgiveness over her past mistake? No, no, she felt she could honestly say she had gratefully accepted His forgiveness.

Was it that she still wanted her own will in choosing her future mate?

No. As much as she admired Eric—perhaps even loved him—she had not been willing to go ahead with plans unless she felt God's approval.

Suddenly, the thought catching her totally off guard, Christine saw what she was clutching tightly. It was the North. But surely He wouldn't ask her to give that up. There was nothing wrong with the North. She loved it. She felt she could even be of service there. Surely that was not wrong. . . .

"Toss it at my feet," she felt God whispering to her heart.

I can't, Lord, she started to answer and then heard again her own voice of days past: *"He's acting like a baby."*

Christine gave herself a mental whack. *Give it up. It's not worth hanging on to it and missing out on God's best.*

But all my hopes, my dreams, my love?

"Throw it down."

Christine opened her hand and held it upright—empty.

Her admission—her agreement to let it go.

In spite of the tears that followed, she had never felt such overwhelming peace.

"Christine," a soft voice seemed to whisper, *"If I want you in the North, don't you think I can take you there? You don't need to work it out. Trust me. And if not the North, don't you think I could give you contentment—peace—even joy—wherever I ask you to go?"*

Christine nodded. God seemed so close. She wondered momentarily if Moses had felt the same sense of His presence as he tossed down his rod.

"Now," God seemed to say. *"What's your hesitation in accepting this young man?"*

To Christine's amazement, she had no answer. There didn't seem to be any reason at all. There was no reason why Eric, who shared her faith and her sense of God's purpose for life, should be turned away simply because she could not see him as part of her North. He was a fine young man. One dedicated to his God, his family, and his patients. Not only that, but he had gained her respect—her heart, yes, her love—with his kindness and integrity. She couldn't believe that she had struggled so long over something so simple. Perhaps the battle had not been over Eric at all but was, in fact, over the issue of who or what had priority in her life. Now that she had relinquished her own plans and dreams and was willing to allow God to control her future, she felt totally at peace. She had her answer.

Eric called the next afternoon. "I am free for the next four hours. Can we talk?"

Christine agreed, anxious to see him.

But she wasn't without concern. She now knew how she felt. Had Eric reached the same conclusion? With a bit of a struggle, Christine was finally able to give up that question to God as well. If Eric had not, that was God's plan and she would accept it. Somehow He would get her through the disappointment. She was His child. She would trust Him.

There was nothing about Eric's demeanor that indicated his direction one way or the other. He was polite, as always, but not more intimate than he had been before.

"How about a walk along the river?" he suggested, and Christine agreed.

"You might want a sweater. There's not much sunshine today."

Christine went for her sweater, informing her aunt that she would be out for a while, and they set out.

"How did your week go?" There was more meaning in his words than a social question.

"I . . . I learned a lot." She smiled. "Mostly from Moses."

"Moses? My lessons were from the apostle Paul."

He picked up a smooth stone and skipped it across the water. Christine remembered Henry doing that. He never seemed to be able to walk near water without skipping stones.

"I would love to hear all about your lessons. Shall we discuss them first—or after?"

"After?" queried Christine.

"After we decide if we are to continue seeing one another."

He skipped another stone, not looking at her.

Christine was hesitant. "I . . . I'm not sure." She wondered if they would still be speaking . . . after.

"Let's wait until after. I'm rather anxious. . . ." He did not continue. Christine wondered if he felt as agitated as she did. He turned from the flowing water to give her his full attention. She could see a tightness in his jaw, and his eyes were serious.

"One thing I learned was about drawing lots," he said.

Christine frowned. Surely he wasn't suggesting they toss a coin to determine their future.

"Well . . . more like a vote than a lot perhaps."

"A vote?"

"A secret ballot. I'm wondering if you are worried that whatever one of us has decided might influence the other."

"I thought of it."

He indicated a bench at the side of the trail, and she understood and let him guide her to a seat. Ducks swam up to the shore, expecting a treat. When one was not forthcoming, they scolded loudly.

"So I thought maybe, to be sure that doesn't happen, we should each write our answer on a piece of paper, then exchange them and unfold them together."

It seemed rather like a childish game, but Christine nodded.

"Have you made up your mind? It's important that we are sure," he said, looking at her intently.

"I feel God has given me direction . . . yes," she answered, feeling suddenly shy.

"Okay—here's the question so we both know exactly what we are answering. 'Do you feel God has given His okay for us to pursue a relationship?' Yes—if you feel He has. No, if you don't. All right?"

"I understand."

He handed her a prepared slip of paper. The question was even penned at the top so that there could be no misunderstanding. "A pencil?"

Christine smiled. "You did come prepared," was her attempt to joke even though she felt a nervousness tightening her stomach.

They turned their backs to each other and wrote out their answers. When Christine turned around she held her breath. She was now committed. Whatever his paper said, hers was already written in black and white.

"All right, let's exchange," he said as he slid a little closer. "On the count of three."

Christine squeezed tight her eyes. She wasn't sure she could look.

"One. Two. Three," he counted, and she unfolded his paper. There was the one word, in big, bold capitals, YES. She closed her eyes again, her heart whispering her gratitude to God.

She heard his whispered, "Thank you, God," and opened her eyes. Her paper was directly in front of him with her longhand "Yes" making a light on his face that touched her deeply.

He placed a finger under her chin and lifted her face toward his. She had never seen him so serious. "We need to talk . . . and talk . . . and talk," he whispered. "I want to know . . . everything . . . about you." His arm slid around her shoulders, drawing her close. His blue eyes, serious and inviting, were very near her own. "So where do we start?" He smiled. "I don't suppose we need to be in a particular hurry. We'll have an entire lifetime—but even then I'm not sure it will be long enough."

She felt tears on her cheek, but she was not sure if they were hers—or his.

Neither of them was aware when the ducks finally gave up their begging and swam away.